THE PACT

Monica McKayhan

THE PACT

An INDIGO Novel

KIMANI
tru
™

THE PACT

ISBN-13: 978-0-373-83093-0
ISBN-10:   0-373-83093-9

© 2008 by Monica McKayhan

www.KimaniTRU.com

Printed in U.S.A.

Acknowledgment

God is the source of my talent and blessings.

To my sons, who took me back to being a teenager for the sake of the Indigo Summer series. To Mark, who is my inspiration.

I'd like to give a special shout-out to a few young people who have made a difference in my life: the Real Talk Teen Book Club in Atlanta (Jim and Jade, Jenaun, Derrick, Alysia, Kenya and Makayla). I will miss you! Thanks to my daughter, Damarka, and my niece, Keya McGathy, for your love and support. Oliver Williams IV and Laveta Ware (teen editors for *Real Talk Teen Newsletter*); you are awesome! And the young people all over the country who have read and loved Indigo Summer…keep reading.

Teen-fiction authors Joyce E. Davis, Earl Sewell and Cecil Cross: it's been a pleasure sharing this YA platform with you. The minds of our youth depend on the voices in fiction that Kimani TRU books represent, so let's keep bringing it to our young people.

chapter 1

Indigo

FINAL Exam.

The last five questions on the test were trick questions. *Miss Harris thinks she's slick,* I thought as I gnawed on the eraser of my number-two pencil. I'd studied hard for this test but now was doubting my answers. I glanced at the clock on the wall, the one with the big black numbers and the second hand that you could actually hear ticking. The second hand seemed to be moving at a faster pace than usual, and I was running out of time. Some of the questions on the test offered a list of multiple choice answers, and I was able to use the process of elimination on them. But others required a specific answer, and those were tricky.

To make things worse, in the middle of the test, my mind started drifting to thoughts of Marcus. It was the last day of school, and the beginning of summer vacation, and Marcus and I were both going away for the summer—separate vacations. He was going to visit his mother in Houston and I was bound for Chicago to spend the summer with my grandmother Nana Summer. Marcus and I would be away from each other for two whole months and some change, and the thought of it was bittersweet. On the one hand, I couldn't wait to see Nana Summer again and spend some time with my cousins in Chicago. But on the other hand, it was going to be hard not seeing Marcus every day, going to the movies or for a bite to eat at Sonic Drive-in. I would miss riding to school with Marcus every morning, tossing my books into the backseat of his Jeep and kicking my feet up on his dash, only to hear him threaten to put me out if I didn't take them down. I would miss our trips to the old airport to watch the rickety planes land, and to count the stars and look for the Big Dipper. Most of all, though, I would miss Marcus's smile and his Jolly Rancher-flavored kisses. Two months would be like two years.

As I approached the last question on the exam, I glanced at the clock on the wall once more. The bell would be ringing soon, and I'd have to turn in my exam, despite my bogus answers to the five questions that weren't multiple choice. Even if I got them wrong, I'd still wind up with at least a C, I thought—maybe a low C, but a C nonetheless. And that was better than a D any day of the week. The last time I'd brought a D home, I'd been on punishment for two weeks and had my cell phone and TV privileges taken away. That was not fun, and I definitely didn't need those kinds of problems now—not at the beginning of my summer vacation. Even though I was headed to Chicago and my parents wouldn't receive my final grades for a few weeks, they would still find a way of making my life miserable if my grades weren't up to par. I would pay one way or another.

"Okay, ladies and gentlemen, I need for you to turn your exams facedown on your desks," said Miss Harris, "and I will come around and pick them up. You will receive your final grades in the mail. Good luck to you all, and have a wonderful summer vacation!"

As the bell sounded, students rushed from their seats and out the door. I took my time about stuffing my book into my backpack. I threw it across my shoulder and stood, sort of moped toward the door.

"Indigo, what's the matter?" Miss Harris asked, cocking her head to the side as if she was trying to read my thoughts.

"I just hope I did okay," I said. "There were a few tricky ones on there."

"You shouldn't worry. You know this stuff. We've gone over it a million times."

"I thought I knew, but some of them had me stumped."

"You'll do fine." She placed her hand on my shoulder. "Have a great summer, Indigo. Your freshman year is over. You'll be a sophomore next year."

She smiled, and I thought about what she'd said. I'd be a sophomore next year. That had a nice ring to it. Meant that I was closer to being a grown-up. It was nice graduating from being a lowly freshman and being at the bottom of the totem pole. You got no respect at the bottom. But as a sophomore, you could push the little people around, and next year, I could do just that. I couldn't wait.

"Thank you, Miss Harris. You have a great summer, too."

I stepped out into the hallway as kids rushed to

their lockers, grabbed the few things that were left in them and headed toward the buses.

Let the summer begin!

I waited out front for Marcus until he finally approached, running his mouth with a couple of his friends from the basketball team. They gave each other high fives and bid each other farewell for the summer. Then Marcus headed my way.

"Ready?" he asked.

"Been standing here all day," I said, and then wrapped my arms around his waist. "What took you so long?"

"I had to say goodbye to some teachers and some of my friends. You know how it is when you're popular and good-looking." He laughed as he unlocked the passenger door of his Jeep and opened it for me.

"Whatever, Marcus." I laughed, too, as I hopped into the passenger's seat and pulled the seat belt across my waist. Marcus jumped into the driver's seat.

"Wanna go to the airport and talk?" I asked.

"Talk about what?" he asked. "I thought we would run by the mall so I could pick up those Jordans I been eyeballin'."

"We need to talk about what we're gonna do this

summer," I said. "You know, we're both going away. Remember?"

"Okay, so we're both going away. And?" Marcus started his Jeep and let the power windows down. Since there was no air-conditioning, we hoped for just the smallest breeze as we sat there in the school's parking lot.

"And we need to decide what we're gonna do."

"Do about what, Indi? I'm not following what you're saying."

I twisted in my seat, wiped sweat from my forehead. I had already thought this through over the past few weeks. Marcus would be heading to Houston, where I was sure there would be lots of pretty girls all up in his face. And I was heading to Chicago to visit Nana. There was a boy there— Jordan Fisher—who had lived around the corner from Nana for as long as I could remember. I would see him sometimes when I visited during spring break or during the few summers that I spent with Nana. He gave me a ring once—one that he got out of the bubble-gum machine at Jewel's drugstore when I was seven years old. The ring meant that I was his girlfriend, but only during my short visit. After that, I'd forgotten all about Jordan—at least until the next time I saw him. He was sort of a "pretend boyfriend" or "summer boyfriend." We had promised to always be together whenever I visited Chicago, with no strings attached once I returned to Atlanta.

I kept thinking that I might bump into Jordan while I was there. Or maybe I'd bump into someone else who would make my summer worthwhile. I wouldn't have any fun if Marcus and I decided to stay committed to each other. We'd both spend the entire summer wondering what the other was doing, and I wasn't up for that. I had to convince Marcus that breaking up—just for a few months—was the best thing to do. It would only be temporary, and at the end of the summer, it would be as if we'd never missed a beat. Things would go back to being just the way they were.

"Can we drive? It's too hot to just sit here. I got sweat pouring down my face," I said.

Marcus tightened his seat belt around his waist and then pulled out of the school's parking lot. He headed toward the small airport—the place where we went to have serious conversations, or to simply watch the sunset or find the Big Dipper amongst the stars. The old airport was the place that Marcus's dad used to take him when he was a little boy, to teach him about manly things and about life. It was the place where Marcus went to clear his head and spend some quiet time with himself. It was a special place.

During the drive he slipped in a CD and T.I.'s voice rang through the speakers. T.I. was one of my favorite artists. In fact, it was my CD. I had picked it up at Stonecrest Mall the day it was released. Marcus had jacked me for it. I let him borrow it once, and he never gave it back. But I never said anything because I'd lost count of the CDs I'd borrowed from him and never given back. The way I figured it, whatever Marcus had, I had, too...and vice versa. If I needed lunch money, he had my back. And I always slipped a package of M&M's into his backpack. That was his favorite candy.

I bounced my shoulders to the music and peered out my window as Marcus pulled into the airport parking lot.

"Okay, here we are," he said, and shrugged.

I was the first to jump out of my seat, hopping out of the Jeep.

"Wanna race?" I asked, and then took off running.

"Not really" was Marcus's response, but he took off running, too.

When Marcus finally caught up, he wrapped his arms around my waist from behind.

"So what's up with you, girl?" he whispered in my ear. "What is all this talk about the summer?"

"The summer is three months, Marcus." I turned to face him. "You'll be gone to Houston, and I'll be in Chicago."

"What's your point?"

"My point is, you might meet someone in Houston that you like better."

He started laughing.

"What's funny? This is not a joke, Marcus. I'm serious."

"You might meet someone in Chicago that you like better."

"So what are you saying?"

"What are you saying?"

"Maybe we should break up just in case."

"Are you serious?"

"Only for a few months, until we come back," I suggested. "If we meet someone new, we won't feel bad about hanging out with them. If we don't meet anyone, and we still feel the same way about each other when we come back, then we get back together."

Marcus stared at me for a moment, waiting for

me to laugh or say I was joking. After realizing I was serious, he turned away, picked up a few rocks. Threw one across the field. The rock hit the ground with a thump, and he threw another one.

"Are you trying to hook up with someone else for the summer?" he finally asked. "Is that what it is, Indi?"

"No, not anyone in particular, Marcus, but you never know."

"That's cool, Indi. If that's what you want."

"Marcus, three months is a long time." Why didn't he understand?

"Two and a half months," he corrected me. "But that's cool. If you think you can't be faithful for that long, then we can break up. No problem."

"Why you gotta make it sound like that?"

"Make it sound like what?"

"Like it's the end of the world."

"Well, if it's not, then what is it?"

"It's just a pact, Marcus," I said. "We make a pact to break up for the summer. If we don't meet anyone new while we're gone, then we'll hook up again when we come back."

"And what if we do meet someone we like, Indi? What then?"

"Then..." I didn't know what then. I hadn't

thought that part through. "If we meet someone new that we like better…then I guess we weren't meant to be."

"Is that so?" he asked. "Is that what you really want, Indi?"

I thought for a moment. I knew that I was still a teenager, still had my whole life ahead of me. It wasn't like we were married or anything, Marcus and I. And I was too young to be tied down or to spend my summer worried about what he was doing…or worse, limiting my fun. I wanted to be young and free.

"Yes, that's what I want." I said the words, but I hoped that I really meant them, because there was no turning back.

"That's fine, Indi." Marcus headed toward his Jeep. "But don't expect me to wait around for you. Let's go. I gotta get to the mall before it's too late. And then I gotta get home and get packed. I have an early flight in the morning."

I silently followed Marcus to his Jeep. He was mad. I could tell, because there were no more words spoken on the way home. I wondered if I had made a mistake by suggesting the pact. Wondered if I would lose my boyfriend forever.

chapter 2

Marcus

The headphones from my iPod rested snugly in my ears, and I stared out the window as the plane floated through the clouds. Thoughts of Indigo rushed through my head as I replayed our pact over and over again. *She's planning on meeting someone else,* I thought, *just as soon as she gets to Chicago.* It seemed as though she wanted to break free, explore her options. As if our relationship meant nothing to her. One thing was for sure, this was her choice, not mine. But I just went with it. I was used to girls changing their minds—switching gears in midstream. The same thing had happened when I'd moved from Stone Mountain to East Point. Kim Porter was the girl who broke up with me the same day she found out that I was moving to the South Side.

"It's too hard trying to go out with somebody at another school, Marcus," she'd said. "Let's just be friends."

Those four words had pierced my heart, and now Indigo was saying pretty much the same thing. Although there was a bright side—there was a chance that she would return to me and still be my girl at the end of the summer. And even though I made her believe that I might not be around, that was all I could hope for.

The flight attendant handed me the Cherry Coke that I'd ordered, and a package of peanuts.

"Thanks," I said, and started flipping through my *Sports Illustrated* magazine. I was reading an article, but I wasn't really comprehending the words. My mind was elsewhere—a million miles away. Just like the plane that was shooting through the clouds and hitting turbulence every few minutes. I looked out the window but could only see white pillows in the sky. Wondered if I was in Indigo's thoughts like she was in mine.

I hadn't even bothered to open my blinds last night when she threw Skittles at my window. She lived next door, and her bedroom window was directly across from mine. When we wanted to get each other's attention, we threw Skittles, or whatever miniature pieces of candy we had readily available, like M&M's or Runts. We always said good-night to each other, no matter what. If I worked late, she waited up for me. Or if she was out late with her family, I'd wait for her. That was just the way it was with Indigo and me. Seeing her face before I went to sleep at night meant that she would find her way into my dreams. However, last night I didn't want her in my dreams.

Mom met me at the baggage-claim area. Her hair, which had once been long and brushing her shoulders, was now in a short, sassy style. I barely recognized her as she approached wearing a short summer dress—a dress that was way too short for somebody's mother to be wearing. I wasn't feeling it at all, and looked around to see if any dudes were looking at her. Her skin was the color of a penny, smooth and silky, and her smile was still very beautiful.

"Marco," she said, and hugged me.

"Hey, Ma. What's up?"

"Boy, I swear you have gotten taller." She smiled

and stepped back to get a good look at me. "Oh, Marco, you're so handsome."

I stood at least two inches taller than my mother and was able to look down at the top of her head.

"I think you've gotten shorter." I laughed.

"Don't be silly. And don't think that because you're taller I can't still beat your butt." She looked at me sideways.

"I wasn't thinking that, Ma."

"You'd better not," she said. "Come on, let's get your bags. How many you got?"

"Two." I walked over to the carousel where people's luggage spun around on the belt. "You look good, Ma."

"Thank you, sweetie." She kissed my forehead. "What's your old daddy up to?"

"Just managing properties. And taking his pickup truck apart every day, only to put it back together again."

We both laughed.

"That Rufus is something else," Ma said. "What about Gloria? How's she doing?"

She asked about Gloria, my father's wife and my stepmother. I was sure she didn't really care how Gloria was doing but asked out of courtesy.

"She's all right," I said, and pulled one of my bags off the carousel. "She's just Gloria."

"The two of you getting along better, Marcus?"

"Not really. I just tolerate her," I said, and thought about our bumpy road, Gloria's and mine. I didn't really care for Gloria, and couldn't stand her cooking. I thought she was only with my father to spend his money and to make my life miserable. Even though I had long ago stopped hoping my parents would get back together, I tolerated Gloria for my pop's sake.

"You don't have to like her, but you have to respect her." My mom rubbed her hand over the waves in my hair.

"I know, Ma. I do respect her," I said, and grabbed my second bag from the carousel.

"That's good. Always respect your elders." She took my carry-on duffel bag from my shoulder and put it on hers. "You ready?"

"I'm ready."

We drove through the streets of Houston's midtown area in Mom's silver convertible BMW, the sunshine beaming down on my forehead. I could just picture myself driving this fly car downtown on a Friday or Saturday night or fifty miles to the beach in Galveston—styling and profiling like it belonged to me.

"You wanna drive?"

It was like she'd read my mind. She pulled over into a McDonald's parking lot.

"I thought you'd never ask." I grinned and did a pimp walk over to the driver's side of the car.

"You know how to drive a stick, Marcus?"

"Yes, ma'am. I sure do." I put the car in second gear, and before she could say another word, I breezed out of the parking lot and back onto the main road.

We cruised the streets, sightseeing, and Mom pointed out what she considered to be all the good restaurants. We drove past the Toyota Center, home of the Houston Rockets basketball team.

"Turn left up here at the light."

I turned and my mother led me into her condominium neighborhood, with multicolored flowers in the front, a huge tennis court and an Olympic-size swimming pool. The pool area was packed, and I couldn't wait to change into my trunks and go for a swim. I pulled the BMW into an empty parking space and popped the trunk. Grabbed my bags and followed Mom up a flight of stairs and into her unit.

"Here we are," she said, unlocking the door.

The house smelled like fresh flowers and Creole food. I had been hoping that mom had prepared something good to eat, because it had been a long time since I'd tasted a good home-cooked meal. My stepmother, Gloria, didn't know the first thing about cooking, and eating at Burger King or McDonald's was getting pretty old. I missed my mother's New Orleans–style cooking, and I was sure my pop did, too—he just didn't want to admit it.

"I made your favorites, baby." Mom headed toward the kitchen and I followed. "Shrimp étoufée and crawfish corn bread."

"You remembered." My mouth watered at the sight of it.

I immediately washed my hands, grabbed a plate from the shelf and dug in.

"Of course I remembered. Boy, you're my child. I know what you like." She laughed.

Mom disappeared into one of the back rooms. I sat at the bar in the kitchen and ate like there was no tomorrow. I grabbed the remote control and turned on the television, flipped the channel to ESPN. I glanced around the room at all the nice art on the walls, lots of photos on the mantel, plants in every corner of the room and candles everywhere. I could just imagine watching a football game on that big-screen television. I almost wished it was still football season.

Pretty soon, my mother came back into the room dressed in a blue business suit.

"Where you going?" I asked.

"I have to go back to the office for a little bit, sweetie. Eat as much as you want. I picked up all your favorites at the store…Twinkies, Cherry Coke, barbecue potato chips," she said. "I even picked up a few of your silly movies from Blockbuster."

"I might go for a swim in a little bit."

"That sounds like fun." She kissed my forehead. "Lots of pretty girls over there at the pool."

Suddenly, thoughts of Indigo rushed through my head again, even though I didn't want her there. I hadn't thought of her since I'd fallen asleep on the plane, but now she was invading my space again. My mother laid a silver key on the countertop next to my plate.

"Here's a key. Make sure you lock the door if you decide to go for a swim," she said. "I'll be home around five."

"Okay, Ma."

"Pick either of the bedrooms you want, Marcus. Just make yourself at home."

I finished eating, rinsed my dishes and placed them in the dishwasher. The kitchen was so clean that I wanted to make sure I left it that way. Mom always was extremely tidy. She took cleanliness to a whole new level; used to drive me crazy when I was small, the way she insisted that I keep my room clean. It almost seemed abnormal. Pop was different. His only requirement was that I pick up after myself. He didn't care if the place was spotless or not.

I decided to explore the two bedrooms and pick the one that I wanted to make my home in. The first one was sort of girly, with floral curtains and a floral bedspread to match. There were lots of candles around the room and a plant on the dresser. It even smelled like roses. I wasn't feeling that room at all. I moved on to the second bedroom—this one was a little more masculine, decorated in blue and white abstract designs. Not nearly as many candles and no plants at all. This was definitely the one for me.

I lifted the miniblinds in the room to let the sunshine in, and to my surprise, the room overlooked the swimming pool. I was able to see everything, from the girl in the yellow bikini about to take a dive into the pool, to the beautiful chocolate girl with long black hair, wearing a tight red T-shirt with LIFEGUARD written across the front of her chest in bold white letters. A girl lifeguard?

I was mesmerized by her beauty; couldn't take my eyes off her. She blew her whistle and yelled at a couple of kids who were playing around in the water. I couldn't hear what she was saying, but I could tell that she made them get out and go to the kiddie pool. When she walked back toward her lifeguard chair, I watched as her booty wobbled in the little white shorts she had on. She was sexy, and something inside me wanted to know who she was.

I rushed into the living room and grabbed my luggage, dragged it into my bedroom. Threw my bag onto the bed, unzipped it and began to search for my swimming trunks. Once I found them, I slipped them on, sprayed a little cologne on and flexed in the mirror. I hadn't worked out in a couple of weeks, and I could tell as my reflection stared back at me. This was no time to be slacking on my weight lifting. I had to get back into the gym as soon as possible. And I would, just as soon as I got back from my swim. I had already peeped the small gymnasium in the lower level of Mom's building and noticed that it had a treadmill and a few free weights. I would definitely have to pay a visit.

I ran a brush across my waves, slipped my flip-flops onto my feet and headed for the water. I walked into the pool area, a towel thrown across my shoulder, and looked around at all the teenagers who were hanging out there. It was a beautiful scene. *This might not be a bad summer after all,* I thought as I tossed my towel onto a chair and removed my flip-flops. I climbed the stairs that led to the diving board, walked to the edge of the board, bounced a couple of times and then dove into the water. The water was cool and refreshing as I swam to the opposite end of the pool. I lifted my head out of the water, rubbed my eyes and noticed Miss Lifeguard taking a quick peek as she sat in her chair with her legs crossed. She didn't think I saw her checking me out. I smiled, but she didn't. Instead, she rolled her eyes and looked the other way. I decided to ignore her for the rest of the afternoon. Ignoring a pretty girl was the surest way of getting her attention. It usually worked like a charm.

"Hi. Are you Marcus?"

As I pulled myself out of the water, a tall, lanky girl with thick glasses stood at the edge of the pool. She wore a one-piece green and white bathing suit, and when she smiled her silver braces sparkled in the sunshine.

"Yeah, I'm Marcus."

"My mom and your mom are friends. We live right across the hall. I'm Michelle."

"Oh, that's cool. Nice to meet you," I said.

"You're visiting here from Atlanta." It was more a statement than a question.

"Yep."

"That's where T.I. and Usher are from. You ever see them around—like at the mall and stuff?"

"Um, I saw Usher a few times at Lenox Square Mall. And I saw T.I. at a Hawks game once. But that's about it."

She was nice, but I really wasn't in the mood for all the chitchat. My eyes were set on a particular life-guard.

"I've lived here for three years…not in Houston, but in this condominium subdivision, that is. I've lived in Houston since I was three." She started answering questions that I hadn't even asked. "Are you thinking of moving here, Marcus?"

"I hadn't really thought about it."

"Your mom says that you are. She says you might be going to school here," she said. "The school is pretty cool. Lots of Hispanics and a few white kids—"

"I'm probably going back to Atlanta at the end

of the summer." I cut her off before she got carried away telling me about a school that didn't interest me one bit.

"Well, if you decide to stay, I'll show you around, okay?"

"Cool."

"You see the girl over there in the yellow bikini?" she asked.

I nodded.

"That's Veronica. Everyone calls her Ronni. Her father's a doctor, and she thinks she's all that... drives a drop-top Pontiac Sunfire." She scanned the pool area. "Don't tell her anything that you don't want repeated."

"I'll remember that." I plopped down onto a lawn chair. Michelle took one beside me.

"You see that guy over there in the red trunks, tall guy with the fresh haircut? That's Aaron. His mother is a counselor at our school. He had to drop out last year because he got arrested for possession of marijuana. Now he goes to an alternative school...."

Michelle continued to tell me the life stories of all the kids at the pool. Made me wonder what her story was—she wasn't so quick to share that information.

"What about the lifeguard over there?" I finally asked the burning question of the day. "Who is she?"

She glared as she looked in the direction of the lifeguard chair, propped her hands behind her head and made herself comfortable before answering.

"Oh, that's Rena." She frowned. "You think she's pretty?"

That was a dumb question. It was as if she was testing me to see what my response would be, sort of like the trick questions that teachers put on tests. Anyone with eyes could see that she was pretty. Even Michelle.

"Yeah, she's pretty."

"Everyone thinks that about her. She's not all that, though," Michelle said, and then dismissed the conversation altogether, moved on with her introductions.

I stole another glance at Rena while she wasn't looking, took in her beauty. As hard as she tried not to look my way, her eyes finally met mine. I smiled, and she actually smiled back. It might not be that hard to get her attention after all.

chapter 3

Indigo

I could see the Navy Pier from the highway as my father's pickup made its way into Chi-town. Chi-town is what we called Daddy's hometown of Chicago. Whenever he brought me into the city, he felt obligated to give me a grand tour, pointing out the landmarks like Grant Park and the Art Institute. He always took me for a drive through the Ida B. Wells projects, the place where he grew up as a kid. Even though the projects had been rehabbed—and he almost didn't recognize them anymore—he had to give me the grand tour anyway. He took the scenic route through downtown Chicago just so I could take in the Magnificent Mile, a place where thousands of people spent their money shopping.

I was so happy when we finally made our way toward Forty-seventh Street, on the south side, where Nana had lived in a two-story brick house since before I was born. As we drove through the neighborhood, a group of boys shot hoops on an old rusty basketball goal. I quickly scanned the crowd, just to see if there were any cute ones in the bunch. There was only one, and when his eyes met mine, I smiled. He smiled back, and Daddy frowned. I pulled down the visor and checked my reflection in the mirror; wanted to make sure I didn't have any drool in the corner of my mouth. After all, I'd been asleep since the moment we reached the mountains in Tennessee. I vaguely remembered waking up for just a moment as we passed by the Tennessee Titans stadium in Nashville. And I could've sworn that Daddy woke me up when we reached Paducah, Kentucky, just to ask me if I wanted a burger from Steak 'n Shake. I remembered being more sleepy than hungry.

When the wheels of Daddy's truck brushed the curb in front of Nana's house, there were tons of people on the porch laughing, partying and having a good time. An old James Brown song was playing loudly. Daddy started singing the lyrics, something about making it funky. My uncles, aunts and cousins were having the time of their lives, everyone engaged in conversations trying to be heard over the music. It wasn't as if the neighbors cared, because some of them were on Nana's porch, too. I hopped out of the front seat of Daddy's truck and stood at the curb for a moment, took a quick glance at the porch to see who was there. When my cousin Little Keith spotted me, he leaped from the porch and rushed toward the truck. He had a Blow Pop in his mouth and held a package of Skittles tightly in his fist.

"Indi!" He hugged me around the waist. "I thought you'd never get here!"

He'd probably been waiting all day.

"What's up, knucklehead?" I asked, and knew he would get on my nerves before the night was over. He always did. "Gimme some of those Skittles."

He loosened his grip on the candy and I emptied them into my palm.

"God, don't take all of 'em!" he said.

"Shut up. They're bad for your teeth, anyway." I popped Little Keith upside his head. "That's why your teeth are rotten as it is."

"Indi!" Daddy gave me a look that said to behave.

"Nana's been waiting forever for you. She made your favorite…macaroni and cheese."

"Little Keith, how you doing?" Daddy asked as he pulled my suitcase from the back of the truck. I had everything I could think of, packed into one suitcase and an overnight bag. I had all my CDs stuffed into my Louis Vuitton backpack: Chris Brown, Ne-Yo, Kanye West and my favorite, Soulja Boy. I fell in love with Soulja Boy when I saw him at the For Sisters Only expo in the fall. That was when I realized that he was much cuter in person than he was on *106 & Park*. Girls were screaming and chasing him all over the Georgia World Congress Center that day at the expo, and I was right there in the midst of the crowd. I could do the Superman Dance better than anybody.

"I'm doing fine, Uncle Harold. Did you bring me something?" Little Keith bounced around. Way too much energy for a Saturday afternoon.

Daddy pretended to pull a silver dollar from behind his ear and then handed it to him. "Something like this?"

"Whoa! This is tight. I gotta go show Nana." He took off running up the stairs into the house.

It didn't take much to impress him, I thought as I made my way up the stairs. I was wearing my Baby Phat jeans, a pink halter top and pink flip-flops to match. I had lip gloss smeared on my lips—the kind Lil Mama sang about in her video. My little Baby Phat purse was stuffed with perfume, eyeliner, a small container of Victoria's Secret lotion, my big hoop earrings, a mood ring that Jade had given me for my sixteenth birthday and a package of peanut M&M's.

Before I could even step onto the porch, I was greeted by my father's cousin Benny, who leaned against the railing with a Budweiser in his hand. His alcohol-scented breath caught me off guard when he got too close.

"Well, if it isn't Indi Bindi Boo." He smiled, revealing spaces in his mouth where teeth should've been. "Loan me twenty dollars, girl."

Everyone on the porch laughed when he said that. His favorite line for everyone he greeted was "Loan me twenty dollars," even though he knew that you were broke. I was definitely broke. The only money I had was the twenty-one dollars that Mama gave me before I left, and hopes of an extra ten Daddy had promised me.

"What you know good, Harold?" Cousin Benny shook my father's hand and passed him a can of beer all in one motion.

"Not a whole lot, Benny. What's going on with you?"

"Just trying to stay above water." He smiled. "Loan me twenty dollars, Harold."

Everyone on the porch roared with laughter again. No doubt, Cousin Benny was the comedian in the family. His wife, Doreen, rocked in a chair on the porch and smiled as I approached. She seemed much prettier when I was smaller. Now she looked as if she had aged, and not gracefully. I remembered spending weekends at their house and sleeping over with their daughter, Sabrina. We would swim in Sabrina's blue and pink plastic pool in their backyard and eat peanut-butter-and-jelly sandwiches for lunch.

"Hey there, Indi. You sure are getting big," Doreen said. "What grade you in now, seventh or eighth?"

"I'm in the tenth grade now." I smiled politely.

"Tenth grade, wow! You're still as pretty as can be," she said. "You and Sabrina used to be so close when you were little. You two are still about the same height...."

"And the same size," Cousin Benny added, "except Sabrina got a little more hips. But you...you built just like a light pole, Indi."

He laughed heartily again, and everyone else did, too. I was embarrassed about my weight being discussed like that—and in front of everyone on the porch as they sat around playing dominoes and drinking Budweisers. Uncle Keith must've recognized the look on my face and rescued me as he swung the front screen door open, grabbed my hand and pulled me inside. Uncle Keith was my favorite relative in the whole family next to Nana. He always made me laugh, and he always had something nice for me, like a silver necklace or a crisp twenty-dollar bill. He was my daddy's younger brother, and they looked almost identical, except Uncle Keith was a little taller—and way cooler. He knew just the right things to say, and he always took me to the coolest places when I was little, like to the lake, to a concert in Washington Park or for a slice of Chicago pizza. He was a lot like Nana—easy to talk to and very wise.

"I thought you might need to be rescued." Uncle Keith smiled and then kissed my cheek, making a farting noise. He tickled me until I begged for mercy.

"How did you know I needed to be rescued?" I asked.

"Uncles know that kinda stuff." He winked. "What you been up to, girl?"

"Nothin' much," I said.

"I want you to meet Debra." He wrapped his arm around the shoulder of a vanilla-colored lady who was standing nearby. "Debra, this is my niece, Indigo."

"It's very nice to meet you, Indi. I've heard so much about you." She smiled. "And Little Keith has been waiting for you all day."

"It's nice to meet you, too," I said, and knew that she wouldn't be around long. Ever since Uncle Keith had gotten a divorce, he always brought women to family gatherings—and always a different one. You never saw one twice. "Where's Nana?"

"She's out back," Uncle Keith said, and then took a drink from his bottle of beer.

I headed for the back patio, where loud music was blasting from the speakers—different music from what was being played on the porch. The people on the front porch listened to old-school tunes, while the folks in the backyard listened to hip-hop. Voices were raised to speak over the music. I took a look around the kitchen at the pans filled with barbecued ribs, chicken, fish and spaghetti. Through the back window, I spotted Nana in the middle of a crowd of people, shaking her hips to the music. She was dancing with my cousin Jimmy, who was teaching her how to do the latest moves. I smiled as I watched her. She had on an outfit I'd rarely seen her in: a pair of blue jeans hugging her hips, a huge T-shirt that read WORLD'S GREATEST GRANDMA across the front and a pair of white Reeboks. She was jazzy, I thought as I crossed my arms across my chest and watched her get jiggy wit' it.

"Indi, what's up?" My cousin Sabrina approached, a toddler attached to her hip. The little girl had a bottle hanging from her lips and a teddy bear pressed tightly against her chest. "You finally made it."

"Yep, I just got here," I said and smiled at my cousin, whose hair was in microbraids and pulled back into a ponytail. When we were little, people thought we were sisters because we looked almost identical. Sabrina had always had the life that I wanted.... She had four brothers, so her house was always lively, with lots of kids to play with. There was always a party at her house. Loud music, drinking and card playing—that was the way I remembered Sabrina's house. And she could literally do whatever she wanted. If she wanted to stay up late, her mother didn't care. If she wanted to stay outside long after the streetlights came on, that was fine, too. She could even have boys over and go places with them before she was twelve years old. That was the life I envied back then. I loved spending the weekends at their house.

My parents were exactly the opposite. There were rules at my house. I wasn't allowed to stay up as long as I wanted to. I actually had a bedtime, and I wasn't allowed to stay out past dark, except on special occasions like the Fourth of July. And as far as boys were concerned, my father was still adjusting to the idea that I had a boyfriend. I *had* a boyfriend, as in past tense. I instantly thought of Marcus. We were officially broken up for the summer, and I missed him already.

It was hard to believe that Sabrina was now a mom at the age of seventeen. Being a mom didn't seem fun at all, especially when you had to take the kid with you everywhere you went. And not only that, Sabrina had to work just to pay a babysitter, and she couldn't go places and do things like she used to—not without finding someone to watch her baby. She didn't even graduate from high school, because she had to get a job when she was in the tenth grade. She was a grown woman inside a teenager's body. I felt a little sorry for her. Not to mention she looked older than seventeen—more like nineteen or twenty.

"Indi, meet my little girl, Brittany," she said. I couldn't help but stare. Brittany was beautiful, with hazel eyes and huge dimples in her cheeks. Her hair was thick and curly. "Brittany, say hello to your cousin Indigo."

"Hi, Brittany." I smiled at the little girl as she laid her head on Sabrina's shoulder, pretending to be shy. "How old is she?"

"She just turned two last month."

"She's so cute."

"She looks like her daddy," Sabrina said. "He's supposed to be coming by here to pick her up. We're not together anymore, but we try to be civil for Brittany's sake. I have a new boyfriend now. You see that guy over there playing dominoes with Uncle Charlie and them? That's my new boo...."

She smiled and pointed toward a card table on the patio, and the guy wearing a red fitted cap with a do-rag underneath looked our way. He smiled and waved and kept staring at me, so much so that it made me uncomfortable. I looked away in order to break the stare.

"His name is Dugan," Sabrina explained, unaware that her so-called new boyfriend was still staring at me. "That's not his real name, though.

His real name is John, but we call him Dugan. Come on, I'll introduce you."

I wasn't really up for meeting Dugan, but I followed her across the lawn anyway. Nana spotted me walking that way and saved me.

"Indi!" She stopped dancing long enough to give me a big hug. "I've been waiting for you, sweet pea."

I missed Nana and couldn't wait for all the guests to leave so that we could catch up on our gossip. I had lots of things to tell her—about school, and about what had gone on in Atlanta since the last time she was there. Nana had become one of my best friends, because she was a good listener and had so much wisdom. I could talk to her about anything, and she always had the right answers.

"When will you be done shaking your groove thing?" I asked.

"Right now," she said. "Excuse me, Jimmy. My special guest has arrived, and we have to go in here and make some corn bread to go with dinner." Nana locked arms with me. "Let's go, sweet pea."

We headed into the kitchen, sat at the old wooden table—the one where I had eaten a million bowls of Froot Loops and Nana and I had talked about everything under the sun. I loved barbecues at Nana's house, and the loud music and laughter that came along with them. I loved catching up with relatives I hadn't seen in ages. But what I loved most of all were the quiet times spent talking with Nana.

chapter 4

Marcus

With my back toward the water, and my eyes toward the sky, I bounced...not once, not twice, but three times on the diving board before plunging into the cool water backward. I did the backstroke across the Olympic-size pool, turned a flip and then ended up at the edge of the pool, face-to-face with the lifeguard. I wiped the excess water from my face and focused.

"What's up?" I asked her, flashing my pearly whites.

"Nothin'," said Rena, and pretended to look away.

"So you work here, huh?" *That was a stupid question*, I thought after it escaped from my lips.

Of course she worked here; any idiot could see that. I tried to redeem myself by asking, "You been a lifeguard long?"

"This is my third summer," she said.

"Cool," I said, and then a long period of dreadful silence followed. I stood there, looking kind of stupid.

"You're a pretty good swimmer," she said.

"Took lessons at the Y when I was younger." I smiled again. "What's your name?"

"Rena. And yours?"

"I'm Marcus Carter," I told Rena. "You live in the neighborhood, right?"

"In the building across from the tennis courts." Her dimples were deep and nice, and I found myself staring into her light brown eyes. "You play tennis, Marcus?"

"No." I frowned. "That's a game for chumps."

"And you say that because…"

"Because I've never seen anyone cool play tennis."

"I play tennis…and I'm very cool," she boasted, "and that's a pretty narrow-minded thing to say, anyway. Usually when people don't know anything about something, they put it down. It's called fear of the unknown."

She sounded like my mother, like she was scolding me or something.

"Is that right?"

"Yes, it is." She looked me square in the eyes. "I can show you how to play."

"Not interested."

Rena climbed down from her lifeguard chair, removed her whistle from around her neck and stuck it in her pocket. "In case you change your mind, you can meet me at the court at seven o'clock."

"You mean tonight?"

"I mean in the morning. Before it gets too hot outside." She removed the clasp that held her ponytail in place and her hair fell to her shoulders. "Will you be there?"

"I doubt it," I said. It wasn't often that I was even awake at 7:00 a.m. during summer vacation. "I'll just be getting my sleep on at seven o'clock in the morning."

"Suit yourself, Marcus," Rena said, and then headed toward the gate. "That's where I'll be in the morning, just in case you change your mind."

Before I could say another word, Rena was gone. I watched as she disappeared through the gate of the pool area and into the parking lot. Part of me wanted to chase her—ask her where she was going, and if she had plans for this evening. I wanted to get to know her, find out what she liked to do, what type of music she liked. I wanted to just look into those light brown eyes a little longer. She had the perfect body—round hips and a nice set of legs, pretty brown skin and perfectly white teeth. Her hair was long and sort of curly. She was the best-looking girl I'd ever seen besides Indigo. And this had been the first time in a long time that I hadn't spent every waking hour thinking of Indigo Summer. Someone had taken my mind off her: Rena was the perfect remedy for a lonely heart.

Suddenly the bass from a bumping 50 Cent song seemed to shake the sidewalk, and I turned to see where the loud music was coming from. A silver Monte Carlo with red leather interior, twenty-twos and tinted windows slowly crept across a speed bump. The driver, sporting braids in his hair and a gold grill at the bottom of his mouth, stuck his head out the window and smiled at Rena. A few words were spoken between them, and then she ran around to the other side, hopped into the passenger's seat and gave the driver a kiss on the lips. He pumped the music louder, turned the car around and then sped out of the parking lot.

"That's Cedric." Michelle was suddenly in my ear again, answering questions, and I hadn't even heard her walk up. "Rena's boyfriend."

"Seems like a nice dude." I grabbed my towel, dried my face and hair. "It was nice to meet you, Michelle. I'll see you around."

I headed toward my mother's building. Took two steps at a time to the second floor, unlocked the door and went inside. After showering and changing into dry clothes, I fixed myself another bowl of étoufée and a tall glass of Cherry Coke. I grabbed the remote to the television, turned to SportsCenter and caught the latest sports news while I ate. My mother's Creole cooking was something that I'd missed. Her New Orleans roots put her in a class by herself when it came to cooking. My stepmother, Gloria's, cooking couldn't compare to my mother's.

New Orleans was a place that I visited in the summertime when I was smaller, and sometimes during Mardi Gras. My grandparents still lived there, even though their home was destroyed in Hurricane Katrina. They moved away to Mississippi just until the city was somewhat rebuilt. It still wasn't complete, in my opinion, but many of the older residents were anxious to get back to the place they considered home. My grandparents refused to call anywhere else their home.

Mom wasn't so quick to move back, but instead had decided to make Houston her home. Houston—a place where a girl named Rena lived. Unfortunately, she had a boyfriend, Cedric, who didn't even seem like her type. Yet she was so comfortable with him. He didn't seem good enough to have a girlfriend so beautiful, but he was the one who drove off with her in the passenger's seat of his Monte Carlo—a very nice Monte Carlo, with nice wheels and a bumping system, I might add. I didn't stand a chance with Rena. She was just a beautiful girl who had temporarily taken my mind off Indigo. I should've known that she was too good to be true.

chapter 5

Indigo

"crank *dat Superman Dance!"*

Every teenager at the barbecue moved to the music of Soulja Boy, doing the Superman Dance in unison. Sabrina, my cousin Kenny and I were in the front row. Little Keith, Bridgette and Shawntay were in the middle and on the back row were my cousin Anjelica, who had just turned twelve, and Uncle Keith. As the other grown-ups looked on, I was surprised to see that Uncle Keith could actually keep up with the rest of us. He knew how to do the Superman Dance just as well as Sabrina and Kenny, who were the best two in the bunch.

I knew the dance very well, because we had rehearsed it in dance practice and had actually talked

Miss Martin, our dance coach, into letting us perform it at halftime at one of our games. Not to mention Jade and I had practiced it a million times on my front porch, even when it was cold outside. Everybody had their own way of doing it and incorporated just a little piece of their own style into it. Some could do it better than others, but everybody was doing it. It was the dance of the century, and if you didn't learn it, then you had to be from Mars or another country.

With a raised shot glass, Cousin Benny tried to mimic our steps. Cousin Doreen raised her can of Colt 45 into the air and cheered us on. Daddy clapped to the music off beat, and Nana just stood by watching with her head cocked to the side. For a minute, I thought she might join us in the middle of the back lawn, but she didn't. She just stood there, with a smile on her face—a smile that let me know she was happy at that moment. Nana was always happy when she could bring the family together for a good time and the police didn't have to come and escort anybody away. I was glad for that, too. Sometimes family gatherings ended in cussing and fighting, or someone drinking too much and causing a scene. But here it was, the sun had gone down—just about dusk, the streetlights were already shining and the crickets were chirping. Lightning bugs were floating through the air, and no one had been arrested. That had to make Nana very happy. I wanted to hug her as I moved my shoulders to the beat.

Later, after everyone had gone home, Sabrina and I moved about the backyard collecting empty beer cans, plastic cups and paper plates and loading them into a huge trash bag. The place was quiet now, except for Daddy and Uncle Keith laughing and talking to each other in lawn chairs on the back patio. They were catching up on old times. It wasn't often that Daddy got to spend time with his brother, considering we lived in Atlanta and only visited Chicago occasionally. At thirty-nine years old, Uncle Keith still lived with Nana. After his divorce from Aunt Pauline, Little Keith's mother, Uncle Keith had moved in with Nana and never left. He'd been depressed and had spent several months trying to recover from the divorce. But even after three years, he was still there, claiming that Nana needed him. However, Nana would have preferred that he get his own place. He drove her crazy most of the time, bringing a different woman home every time she turned around. And he never cleaned up after himself, Nana once told me. It was like raising him all over again, and as far as she could tell, Uncle Keith was a grown man.

As Sabrina and I stood in the kitchen and washed dishes by hand, I noticed that the music had changed from hip-hop back to the oldies. Nana didn't have a dishwasher, only a sink with running water. I covered the huge pan of ribs with aluminum foil and placed the bowl of potato salad into the refrigerator.

"You wanna go out with me tonight, Indi?" Sabrina asked. "I sent Brittany home with my mama and daddy, so I'm as free as a bird."

"Go out where?" I asked.

"There's a club on the South Side of town, and it'll be on and poppin' at about ten o'clock. I can get you in if you wanna go." Sabrina dried her hands with a dish towel. "So what's up?"

"My daddy's still here. And he's not leaving to go back to Atlanta until tomorrow morning. I don't know if he'll let me go," I said. "Nana might not let me go, either."

"Just leave it up to me." Sabrina stood about five feet eleven inches tall—the perfect height for a model. Her shoulder-length hair brushed her bare shoulders, and her halter top hugged her small breasts. Her short denim shorts revealed her long, smooth vanilla legs, and she wore wedge-heeled sandals. Everyone had always compared Sabrina and me to each other—especially when we were smaller. Said that we could pass for sisters. I had to admit, we did favor each other, but I didn't have half the body that Sabrina had. And my legs were nowhere near as shapely as hers.

"What you wearing?" I asked.

"I'm wearing what I got on," she said. "It's a very relaxed environment. You might wanna wear something a little sexier. Don't put it on yet, though. I don't want Nana trippin' before we leave. You can change at my place."

"Your place?" I asked with a raised eyebrow. "You got your own place?"

"Shoot, yeah! I thought you knew," she said. "I'm almost grown now, Indi. I'll be eighteen in a few months. Plus, I got my own kid, so that makes me grown anyway."

"I can't believe you have your own place." I was in awe of my cousin, who I'd always looked up to.

I wanted to be just like Sabrina, wanted to dress like her and wear my hair the same way. And I'd always wanted to act just like her. She seemed to handle things very well, and was smarter than most, with a high grade-point average all through school. The cute boys always wanted to date her, and everybody wanted to be in her circle. She had her own little following when we were little. Sabrina was popular, smart and pretty—all the things that I wanted to be.

When I found out that she was pregnant, I'd been disappointed. I'd always thought she would grow up to be a doctor or a lawyer, or someone who would make important decisions in the world. But instead, she had let her family down by having a baby at a young age and dropping out of high school. She had let me down, too, because I was the one who had looked up to her. Who would I look up to now? Even though she had gotten her GED, it wasn't the same. She was the one who was supposed to do big things.

"Of course I have my own place. It's nothing fancy, just a little apartment. Not much, but it's mine." Sabrina stuffed what was left of the baked beans into the fridge and then turned to me. "Go find something to wear. I'll talk to Cousin Harold and Nana. Don't worry about a thing."

Whatever she said to them must've worked, because before I knew it, we were in Sabrina's boyfriend, Dugan's, fixed-up Caprice Classic. It was tan and had huge wheels and furry seat covers. A big fuzzy pair of dice hung from the rearview mirror.

"This is Dugan's car. I'm just driving it because my car is in the shop. But he's about to buy me that new Escalade, anyway." She smiled as she turned at the stoplight. "He buys me whatever I want. We might be getting married soon."

"Married? For real?"

"Don't tell nobody, because I don't wanna hear their mouths. Everyone will think that I'm too young and that I'm rushing into it."

"Aren't you—too young, I mean?"

"I'll be eighteen soon, Indi. And I won't even need my parents' permission. That's what we're waiting on—my eighteenth birthday." She pulled a package of Newports from over the sun visor. Pulled out a cigarette and lit it. "Enough about me. What's going on with you, girl? I heard you got a little boyfriend down there in Hotlanta."

"I had a boyfriend. His name was Marcus."

"Y'all broke up?"

"Just for the summer," I said. "We made a pact that if we didn't meet anybody new on summer vacation, we would get back together at the end of the summer."

"Girl, whatever! What kinda pact is that?" She laughed and took a puff from her cigarette. "That boy is gonna hook up with somebody else, and so are you! That's the silliest thing I ever heard. Whose crazy idea was that, anyway?"

She turned off the air-conditioning and rolled her window all the way down. I followed her lead and rolled mine down, too, to let the smoke out.

"It was my idea," I admitted, and immediately wanted to change the subject. Didn't want to think about Marcus meeting someone new. I hadn't given much thought to *him* meeting someone new, only the fact that I might. But now, after listening to Sabrina, I realized that there was a good chance Marcus might meet another girl in Houston and actually like her better than me. That thought made my stomach turn flips. I couldn't believe that I hadn't thought this through. I'd only thought of myself the whole time. What if I didn't meet anyone and Marcus ended up with a new girlfriend? Where would that leave me at the end of the summer?

"Earth to Indigo...." Sabrina was trying to get my attention, as I had been lost in thought. She took another drag from her cigarette and then flipped the ashes out the window. "There will be some honeys at the club tonight. You wait and see."

Sabrina turned into an old apartment complex. People were standing around outside, as if a party were going on right there in the parking lot. There was laughter and loud music as we pulled into an empty space. After we stepped out of the car, I followed Sabrina along the sidewalk and up a flight of wooden stairs. She stopped in front of an apartment door—18E—and banged on it.

"Dugan, open the door!" she yelled.

Dugan took his time about opening the door, and when he did, he stood there with a towel wrapped around his waist and nothing else. I observed his huge arms and biceps, and his abs were tight like Marcus's. He was handsome, I thought, as my eyes finally checked out his braids, which were freshly done. The do-rag and fitted cap that he'd worn earlier at Nana's were gone, and I couldn't help noticing that his braids hung to his shoulders. I'd been so busy avoiding his stares earlier at the barbecue, I hadn't noticed that his eyes were hazel colored and his smile was a lot like Chris Brown's. He wrapped his arms around Sabrina to hug her, but his eyes were steady on mine. And the shower gel that he'd just used was tickling my nose.

"You didn't get a chance to meet my cousin Indigo earlier," Sabrina said. "Indigo, this is Dugan— Dugan, Indigo."

"Nice to meet you, Indigo." He held his hand out to me and I shook it. "Come on in and have a seat."

I stepped into the apartment and immediately caught the aroma of some type of berry-smelling incense. Candles burned on the coffee table, and I almost didn't notice the old stained carpet because the leather furniture was so nice. There was a big-screen TV in the corner of the room, tuned to ESPN. A blond announcer interviewed pro basketball player Dwayne Wade.

"What you drinkin', Indi?" Sabrina asked. "You want a beer?"

"No. I'm fine," I said, glancing around at the African art on the stained walls and the beautiful plants that were neatly placed in the corners of the room.

I wondered how my cousin could afford to furnish a place like this, considering she worked at Jewel drugstore part-time. The television alone must've cost a fortune. And leather furniture wasn't cheap. Dugan hit the power on the stereo. I hadn't even noticed it was there until loud music spilled out of it. As Ne-Yo's voice rang through the speakers, Dugan switched the channel to BET and *Hell Date* was on. I watched, but couldn't hear what was being said because the TV was muted.

Sabrina was on the phone with one of her girl-friends, describing what the plans were for the evening.

As I sat on the edge of the leather sofa, I wondered what the rest of the night would bring.

chapter 6

Indigo

The bass from the music pounded in my chest as we stood in line waiting to get into the club. My first real nightclub experience—and I was so nervous. I had been to house parties before, and to teen clubs in Atlanta, but not to a real nightclub that had bouncers and a bar that served alcohol. I was afraid that once I reached the front of the line and the security person at the door took a look at my fake ID, I'd be in trouble. They would know that I wasn't twenty-three years old and that the girl in the photo wasn't really me. They wouldn't hesitate to arrest me and drag my sixteen-year-old behind to the youth detention center and call my father. Or worse, call Nana. That would put an end to my life as I currently knew it. I wouldn't be able to show my face anywhere in the state of Illinois again.

The huge security guard, with arms of steel and a body about the size of Arnold Schwarzenegger's, snatched my ID from my hand. A gun hung on his hip as he took a look at it and then looked at me. He never showed any expression on his face as he stood there for what seemed like a lifetime. My heart pounded, and I wondered if he could hear it. Finally, he handed me the piece of plastic back and nodded toward the entrance.

"Ten bucks at the door," he said.

There was a woman at a booth near the doorway collecting money. I handed her the crumpled ten-dollar bill Sabrina had given me in the car. She grabbed it and said, "Go ahead."

I almost asked if she was sure, but instead I glided inside, Sabrina behind me. The security guard had checked out her ID, demanded that she pay ten dollars and given her the same nod he'd given me.

"Come on, let's find some sucker to buy us a drink." She locked arms with me and we walked into the club. The smell of cigarettes was overwhelming, and instantly my eyes began to water. I'd never smelled so much cigarette smoke in my life.

The lights were dim, and music was so loud that I could feel the bass in my chest. People were having loud conversations so that they could be heard over the music. Sabrina and I pushed our way through the crowd and ended up at the bar. We plopped down onto bar stools, and my eyes veered toward the dance floor, which was so crowded that people were barely able to move. The music got even louder as the deejay pumped a Beyoncé song. With headphones on his ears, Deejay Crunk, as he called himself, moved to the music, too.

"You wanna dance?" A deep voice was in my ear almost before I had blinked.

When I turned to see who it was, I was surprised to find a pair of green eyes looking back at me. He wore sagging jeans and a Sean John shirt. He had a short, fresh haircut, and when he smiled, I could see the gold grill on his teeth. He was cute, I had to admit.

"Yeah" is all I said before hopping off my bar stool.

I handed Sabrina my purse and followed Green Eyes to the dance floor.

"You come here a lot?" he asked as we both began to move to the music.

"First time," I said.

"What?" He was shocked. "This is the place to be. You must live under a rock."

"I live in Atlanta."

"Oh, you from the A?" He smiled. "I knew you weren't from around here. I would've remembered you with your fine self."

"Are you from Chicago?" I asked, just so I could stop blushing.

"South Side...all day long, baby," he said, showing that gold grill again. "How long you gon' be here?"

"I'm here for the summer."

"Cool, maybe I can show you around a little bit."

"Maybe you can," I said, and knew that wouldn't happen. But a girl could pretend, couldn't she?

Within the first hour, at least five guys had offered to show me around Chicago. Two had promised to take me downtown for a slice of Chicago pizza, claiming that it was the best in the world. One of them had invited me to a movie at the Music Box Theatre. And one had asked me to meet him at the Beverly Center on Sunday for a talent show. I doubted that I would be going anywhere with any of them, especially if my grandmother Nana Summer had a say in the matter. I simply smiled and told them to give me their phone numbers so that I could key them into my cell phone. It seemed that I was keying in phone numbers all night.

I found Sabrina in the club's VIP section. She was sipping something with an umbrella in it and motioned for me to join her on a leather sofa.

"Are you okay, Indi?"

"I'm cool," I said. "What are you doing up here?"

"Some of my friends are in a band. They perform here sometimes, and when they're not working, they chill in the VIP," Sabrina explained. "Sometimes R. Kelly even chills up here when he's in town."

"Are you serious?"

"Very…. He might even show up tonight," Sabrina said, "but you gotta be cool when he comes in. Don't be acting like a groupie."

"Have you seen him in here before?"

"Yep, one time he came in with T-Pain, and they sat right there on that sofa over there." She pointed to the leather sofa across from us, where two girls were kissing. Nobody seemed to mind, and I tried not to stare, but I couldn't help it. I'd never seen that type of behavior in a public place before. I'd seen gay people before. They were all over my school. And it wasn't unusual to see them walking down the streets of Atlanta on any given day. But to see a female couple kissing each other on a leather sofa—now, that was a trip. "You want something to drink, Indi?"

The cocktail waitress stood near us, waited for my response.

"No, I'm good."

"Bring her a club soda," Sabrina laughed. "She's still a virgin."

I didn't find her little joke funny, especially since it was true. But I didn't sweat it; I nodded to the waitress and she disappeared. I sat there and continued to people-watch. The over-twenty-one crowd wasn't much different from the youngsters who hung out at the teen club that I had gone to a couple of times in Atlanta. The only real difference that I could see was that at the older club, they served alcohol. The music and dancing was all the same— and guys still hit on me, just like they did at the teen club. The grown-up club was actually pretty cool, I thought as I bounced my head to the sounds of Ne-Yo.

I held the glass filled with club soda in my hand, a cherry floating around in it. It looked as if I was having what Nana referred to as a "highball." I wasn't old enough to drink, but it didn't hurt to pretend that I was as I sipped my virgin highball. I had to admit, it felt pretty good to be in one of the hottest clubs on the South Side of Chicago, in the VIP section with all the important people, sipping what looked like a shot of alcohol and listening to good music. What could be better?

Sabrina knew just about everybody in the place and introduced me to so many people that I couldn't remember any of their names. She kicked her shoes off and relaxed on the sofa as if she were at home. She pulled her Newports out of her purse, lit one and held it between her long, skinny fingers. I watched my older cousin—the girl I had looked up to all my life—and admired her at that moment. She still had it going on, I thought. Even though she'd dropped out of school, had a baby and pretty much pissed her parents off, she still had a great life. She had her own apartment and an older boyfriend, and she was a VIP at one the hottest clubs in Chicago.

It was muggy outside when we stepped into the heat of the night. Sabrina searched for the keys to Dugan's car in her Baby Phat purse. Once she found them, she hit the power locks and we both climbed in.

"You had a good time, Indi?"

"The best," I said, unable to contain my excitement. I wanted to call Jade so badly and tell her about my experience, but it was late—almost two o'clock in the morning and well past both of our bedtimes.

"You hungry?" Sabrina asked.

"A little bit."

Sabrina pulled into the nearest IHOP and we went inside. We ordered plates filled with pancakes, sausages and eggs. After we ate, Sabrina paid the tab and drove us back to her place. When we stepped inside, Dugan was reclining on the sofa, flipping through the channels on the television.

"How was it?" he asked.

"It was cool," Sabrina told him. "I think Indi had a good time. She was on the dance floor all night."

"You had fun, Indi?" Dugan asked.

"Yes," I said.

"I'll get you some pillows and stuff," Sabrina said, and then disappeared into the bedroom.

I took a seat in a chair in the corner of the room. Dugan stole a glance at me, smiled and then zeroed in on a girl shaking her booty in a rap video.

"Can you shake like that?" he asked.

I wasn't really sure what answer he was expecting, but I was happy when Sabrina stepped back into the room carrying a blanket and two pillows.

"Indi, you can sleep on the sofa or you can make a pallet on the floor. Whichever you prefer."

"I'll sleep on the couch."

"Cool," she said. "Let's go, Dugie...so Indi can get to bed."

Dugan followed Sabrina into their bedroom, but not before flashing his pearly whites at me one more time.

"Sweet dreams," he said, and then shut the door.

I grabbed the remote control, turned the television to HBO and found a movie. I climbed onto the sofa, sank my head into the pillow. Before long, my eyelids became too heavy to keep open. The drive from Atlanta to Chicago in Daddy's pickup had taken its toll on me, and I gave in to the sleep that finally took over.

The smell of burned cheese crept across my nose, and I thought I was dreaming. I raised my head and looked into the kitchen. Dugan had the place smoking as he stood near the stove. He caught me looking.

"I didn't mean to wake you up, Indi. I got a little hungry in the middle of the night." He smiled. "You hungry? I make a mean grilled-cheese sandwich."

"Yeah, I'm a little hungry," I said. I wiped sleep from my eyes and went to the kitchen.

A skillet was already smoking on the stove when Dugan grabbed a tub of margarine and a loaf of bread from the refrigerator. He went into the living room and turned on the stereo before returning to melt margarine over a high flame. I took a seat at the kitchen table and watched Dugan cook. I loved watching him, and rested my chin in the palms of my hands.

"You and Brina could pass for sisters, you know. Y'all both have that beautiful smile and that smooth vanilla skin." His fingertips caressed my face.

"Everybody says that."

"That's why I look at you so much. I can't help it. You're so pretty."

I stood and started bouncing to the rhythm of Unk, just to change the vibe in the room. I couldn't tell if Dugan was flirting or if he was just paying me a compliment. Either way, I was uncomfortable and directed my energy in a different direction. As I walked it out, Dugan started walking it out, too. All too quickly, he was in my space—so close I could feel his energy. My heart began to pound, and I wondered if he could hear it thumping underneath the strapless tube top I'd chosen for the club. I wondered if it was the Apple Bottoms jeans that caught his attention. His cologne invaded my nose as he moved to the beat, and his braids were swinging to their own rhythm.

"Let me show you something," Dugan said, and showed me a dance move. "You do it."

I did his dance move, and then he showed me another. Before long, he had me doing an entire routine. I decided to let go of my inhibitions and have fun, and once the Unk song went off we bounced to the sounds of Lil Jon and then Kanye West. And in between moves, Dugan cooked us grilled-cheese sandwiches. He placed both sandwiches on paper plates and poured us each a glass of Hawaiian Punch.

While we ate, we talked about music and hip-hop artists. We debated about who had the hottest CD and which artists we thought would be the most fun to hang out with.

"I could roll with Fifty," Dugan said. "He's cocky, but he would probably be cool to hang out with."

"He's way too cocky." I laughed. "I think I might like to hang with T.I."

"Indi, he won't be able to hang out with you until he gets off house arrest." Dugan laughed. It was no secret that T.I. had legal troubles. He'd been arrested one night before the BET Hip-Hop Awards. I remembered when it had happened because it had almost brought tears to my eyes. I kept telling Jade that he had been set up, and I still believed it. But I was helpless. There was not much his biggest fan could do to relieve him of his troubles—except pray. And I had already done that.

"That's okay, I'll wait for him." Dugan and I both laughed.

"I guess you'll have to hang with Jay-Z instead," Dugan said.

"Nah. Beyoncé might not like that. And I ain't got time to be fighting her over no man."

"But what if he preferred you over her?"

I contemplated Dugan's question, as ridiculous as it was. There was no way on earth Jay-Z would choose me over Beyoncé. She was the beauty queen of hip-hop.

"She got more money, and way more booty." I laughed, but Dugan wasn't laughing.

"You're just as beautiful, though, Indi. For real."

There was that uncomfortable feeling again. And once again I was on the floor dancing to the beats of 50 Cent, a song where Akon was harmonizing in the background. Dugan noticed my discomfort and quietly finished his grilled-cheese sandwich, downed his second glass of Hawaiian Punch. Stood.

"I'll let you get some sleep, girl," he said. "I'm stepping out for a little bit, so maybe I'll see you tomorrow."

"Okay."

"You need anything before I go?"

"No."

"Okay, cool." Dugan walked toward the door.

"Thanks for the sandwich," I said.

"My pleasure." He winked. "Sweet dreams."

The thought of my dreams was what scared me as he left the room. When I heard the front door close, and a key locking it, I became very afraid... afraid that instead of sweet dreams, I might have Dugan dreams.

chapter 7

Marcus

when I heard the tapping noise, I thought I was dreaming. It stopped for a moment and I dozed off again. Just as soon as I began to drift into a nice dream, the tapping started up again. That was when I realized that it was the front door. I looked over at the digital clock on the nightstand. It was nine o'clock. I wiped the sleep from my eyes and hopped out of bed. I peeked into my mom's bedroom. Her bed was neatly made and covered with beige and orange decorative pillows. I made my way into the kitchen, where a stack of pancakes and a few sausage patties sat on a plate on the stove. A note was posted on the refrigerator, held there by a magnet. It read:

Marcus,
I had to go into the office for a bit, but I made
your favorite breakfast. Be home soon. Take
the trash out when you get up.
Love & Kisses,
Mom

I glanced over at the trash bag in the corner, neatly closed with a twist tie. Just as I was reaching for a plate on the shelf, the tapping started again. I had forgotten that someone was at the door. When I looked through the peephole, Michelle's eyes were staring back at me.

"What's up?" I asked as I swung the door open.

"Good morning, Marcus. What you doing?"

"I was sleeping until you started knocking on the door like a crazy person," I said. "You wanna come in or what?"

"Yeah, okay." She stepped inside and shut the door behind her.

"My mother made me pancakes. You want some?"

"Sure, why not?" She plopped down in one of the high chairs at the kitchen bar.

I pulled a couple of plates from the shelf, set one in front of Michelle.

"I'm gonna go wash my face. I'll be right back."

* * *

I stepped into the bathroom and gazed at my reflection in the mirror, then rubbed a warm washcloth across my face. I brushed my teeth and swished mouthwash around in my mouth. When I heard Drew Carey's voice from *The Price Is Right* blasting on the TV in the living room, I knew that Michelle hadn't wasted any time making herself at home. When I stepped back into the kitchen, she had already fixed her plate and was pouring maple syrup on her pancakes.

"Your mom asked me to show you around the city." She grinned. "So where you wanna go?"

"You got a car?" I asked, and began loading my plate down with pancakes and sausage.

"Yeah. It's not anything special, but it's transportation," she said.

"Will it make it to the mall?"

"Of course." She stuffed a forkful of pancakes into her mouth. Syrup dripped down her chin, and she giggled.

I handed Michelle a paper towel so she could wipe her mouth. "Let's go there, then."

"Cool," she said, and almost knocked her glass of orange juice over.

She was clumsy.

* * *

At the mall, I tried to break free from Michelle so that I could check out other girls, but I couldn't. She was on my heels with every step. There were so many cute girls that I couldn't help checking them out. And they were checking me out, too. The next time I visited the mall, it wouldn't be with a nerdy girl like Michelle. She wore a knee-length denim skirt and a dull blue T-shirt with GUESS written across the front of it—something my grandmother would wear to the mall. Her hair was pulled back into a ponytail. Michelle was plain; no guy would even give her a second glance, I thought as we strolled through the mall.

"Marcus, do you play *Madden*?"

"Of course. That's my game."

"Well, let's see what you got!"

Before I could protest, Michelle had pulled me into a video store, grabbed a controller and begun playing *Madden NFL*. I grabbed one, too, and before long we were lost in the game. She was good at it, talking junk just like she was one of my boys. After my team lost, Michelle did the touchdown dance right in the middle of the floor.

"Sorry I had to whip you like that, Marcus." She laughed.

"That was just luck."

"Not luck, boy...skill," she said. "Let's go grab something to eat. You hungry?"

"I could eat." I smiled.

Michelle started cracking up. "You sounded just like Derek Luke in that *Antwone Fisher* movie when you said that.... 'I could eat.' Remember that scene?"

"Of course I remember that scene," I said. "That was one of my favorite movies. He was role-playing with Denzel Washington."

"My favorite movie was *American Gangster*," she said. "Anything with Denzel in it is good."

"*American Gangster* was cool, but the best Denzel movie of all time was *Training Day*...hands down."

"Nah, I didn't like Denzel in that movie. He played a bad guy." Michelle frowned.

"He can't always play a good guy. He has to flex his acting skills a little bit."

"Whatever, Marcus." She laughed. "What you want to eat?"

"A burger is good," I said as we stepped into the food court.

There were so many different restaurants to choose from, with so many types of food to offer. A burger place was always a sure shot, so we stepped into the Burger King line, each ordered a Whopper combo meal and found a table in the center of the court. We talked about everything as we ate—sports, music, movies—everything. Michelle was just like one of the guys, and I'd had a good time at the mall with her.

When I walked into the condo, Mom was in the kitchen, an apron tied around her waist. She was stirring some ground turkey in a pan.

"I hope you're hungry. I'm making tacos, baby," she said.

"I'll be hungry in a little bit." I kissed her cheek. "How was work?"

"It was just work. Nothing special." She pulled a package of taco seasoning from the shelf. "What did you do today?"

"Um, I just went to the mall with Michelle."

"Oh, that's nice. I asked her to show you around a little bit. I hope you don't mind."

"Nah, it was cool." I smiled. "I'm gonna go change. I saw some workout equipment downstairs in the gym. I wanna go down there and pump some iron."

"That's fine, Marcus. But hurry back. Dinner's almost ready."

"Okay, Ma."

* * *

I changed into an old T-shirt and a pair of gym shorts, headed downstairs. The windows of the gymnasium were fogged from the air-conditioning. It was freezing, and I wished I'd worn long sweatpants but knew it wouldn't be long before I was sweating like crazy. I stepped onto the treadmill and began jogging. I had my iPod, and when I put the headphones on, Young Joc began to rap in my ears. After I got my heart rate up, I stopped running and began to briskly walk on the treadmill. Slowed to a less intense pace to cool down and then hopped off the machine to catch my breath. I started stretching my muscles and then stepped over to the free weights side of the room. Just as I began to pump some iron, a familiar face showed up in the gym.

"You stood me up this morning." Rena placed her hands on her hips. She was wearing short, tight gym shorts and a snug top that hugged her breasts.

"Oh, I forgot all about that." I found myself smiling—I couldn't help it. "I told you I don't play tennis, anyway. And especially not at seven o'clock in the morning."

Rena turned away, hopped onto the treadmill, started pressing buttons to set it where she wanted it. Her breasts began to bounce up and down as she started to jog, and I found myself staring at her toned legs as they moved back and forth. Her pink and gray Nikes matched her pink and gray outfit, and she moved to a rhythm all her own.

After I finished pumping weights, I grabbed my towel, threw it over my shoulder and headed for the door.

"Hey, Marcus, can you spot me on the weight bench before you leave?"

I thought about it for a minute, and then said, "Yeah, I can do that."

Rena hopped off the treadmill, wiped sweat from her forehead and headed for the weights. She changed the weights on the barbell and then lay flat on her back. I walked toward the bench, helped her lift the barbell and spotted her as she lifted the weights—up and down, and then up and down again. She breathed and then released with each repetition. She was the first girl I'd ever seen work out this way. The girls on the basketball team at my school lifted weights, but weren't as serious about exercise as Rena was. And most girls didn't want to do anything that would mess up their hair. But it was apparent that Rena did it on a regular basis and that she was disciplined.

After she'd put the weights back where they belonged, she sat up slowly, sweat popping from her forehead. Most girls would die if a boy saw them sweat, but Rena wasn't afraid to get her workout on. It only made her more beautiful, and worse, made me more attracted to her. She grabbed the towel from my shoulder, wiped her face with it and smiled. I didn't even mind that her sweat was all over my towel.

"Thank you, Marcus," she said. "You wanna go to the beach later? It's a nice little drive from here."

"I don't know...." I said. Part of me wanted to explore the beach with Rena, especially since I hadn't been yet. And what could be better than playing in the ocean with a beautiful girl? But the responsible side of me knew that this girl had a boyfriend—and the beach at night was no place to be with someone else's girl.

"Oh, come on...the beach is nice. It's very beautiful at night. You can actually see the stars reflecting off the water. There's nothing like it." She stood, threw my towel back to me. "Meet me out front at eight."

Before I could protest, Rena was gone. I stood there for a moment, watching her walk away. I should've gone after her, told her I wouldn't make it, but I didn't. Instead, I glanced at my watch. It was 6:36. I had exactly one hour and twenty-four minutes to come up with one good excuse for not going to the beach with Rena. But by the time 7:59 rolled around, I didn't have a single excuse.

chapter 8

Marcus

she was ten minutes late, I thought as I glanced at my watch for the third time. I stood in front of the entrance to the pool, pacing back and forth, debating whether I should go back inside, call it a night, watch some BET. I was happy to see Rena heading my way, a colorful beach towel folded in her arms. She'd changed clothes and was wearing a swimsuit cover-up that just barely covered her thighs and was tied around her neck. Underneath, she wore a white bikini that I could see through the flimsy material. A pair of flip-flops on her feet, she walked briskly toward me.

"Sorry I'm late, Marcus."

"I was about to leave," I teased. "I don't have all night to be waiting on you, girl."

"Shut up, Marcus." She grabbed my arm. "Come on. Let's go."

Rena led the way to her little Hyundai Sonata that was parked in the lot. She unlocked the power doors and we both hopped inside. I let my window down to catch a cool breeze as we pulled out of the complex and onto the main road. As we merged onto Interstate 45 headed south, I started messing with the buttons on Rena's radio in search of a hip-hop station.

"Try 104.9, Marcus."

"Thank you," I said, and tuned the radio to 104.9. When I heard Keyshia Cole crooning, I knew it was the right station.

As we got closer to the beach, I could smell the salt water. We parked in a nearby lot, and I was the first to step out of the car. I waited while Rena sat in the car and refreshed her makeup. What was the point of putting on makeup when you were about to go for a swim? I thought about it for a moment but didn't bother to try and understand. It was just one of those silly things that girls did.

When she was finally done, Rena and I walked along a dirt trail that led to the beach, our towels in tow. I was prepared for a nice swim in the ocean, dressed in a pair of swimming trunks and an old

T-shirt. Finally, I could feel the warm sand between my toes and the blue water stretched as far as the eye could see. Jet Skis raced up and down the ocean, and sailboats slowly made their last journeys across the water. It was getting late, and most people were packing things up and heading home.

Rena spread her beach towel out on the sand, and I stretched mine out next to hers. She plopped down and I sat beside her.

"Isn't it beautiful out here, Marcus?"

"It's cool."

"The beach is a very romantic place," she said. "I love coming here."

"You come here very often with your boyfriend?" I asked.

"I don't have a boyfriend," she said.

That wasn't the picture I had. I'd seen her with the dude in the Monte Carlo and he might as well have been wearing a T-shirt that said RENA'S BOY-FRIEND across the front of it. But I let it go, changed the subject.

"So what grade are you in, anyway?" I asked Rena.

"I'll be a senior when school starts. Planning to go to FAMU when I graduate," she said. "What about you, Marcus?"

"I'll be a junior. Thinking about either Yale or Harvard."

"Yale or Harvard? Those are schools for nerds," she said.

"According to who?"

"According to the African-American population, Marcus. News flash…black kids don't go to Harvard or Yale." She laughed. "What about an HBCU like Morehouse or Clark Atlanta?"

"I had a white coach tell me once that I wasn't good enough to go to Harvard or Yale. So it's been my sole purpose in life to prove him wrong. Why can't black kids go to an Ivy League college just like white kids? What makes them better than us?"

"It doesn't make them better than us. It's just the way things are, Marcus. They go to white schools, and we go to black schools," Rena said. "I'm not interested in a school like that. I want to go to a school where I can learn about my heritage…and where other students look like me."

"I hear you," I said, and then stretched out on my beach towel, placed my hands behind my head and gazed into the sky. I was done talking about it, because it was clear that we didn't agree on the subject.

The sun had gone down, and it was beginning to

get dark. The only light was from the moon and the stars. Rena took off her dress, and when it dropped to her ankles, I found myself staring. The bikini covered so little of her body that it should've been against the law to be dressed that way in front of me. She headed for the water, took a swim. I decided to join her. The water felt warm and refreshing as a wave crashed upon the shore. Every few seconds another wave would hit, and I found myself fighting just to stand up. I swam deeper into the ocean, and Rena looked hesitant to join me.

"Come on," I told her.

"Not too far, Marcus," she said. "I'm cool right here."

"Don't tell me you're scared." I moved toward her. "Aren't you a lifeguard?"

"The ocean is different from a swimming pool. It's much deeper," she said, "not to mention it's dark out here."

"Come on, I won't let anything happen to you." I reached for Rena's waist. She was resistant at first. Then she wrapped her arms around my neck and I eased her out into the water.

She pulled closer to me and then buried her face in my neck. It felt like we were slow dancing or something, the way her arms tightened around me, and when the waves knocked up against us it was a struggle just to balance ourselves against them. I lifted her and carried her farther out into the ocean. That was when I noticed how good she smelled, like some bubble-bath products that girls picked up at the mall. As her legs wrapped tightly around my waist, my heart started pounding rapidly. There was no doubt I was attracted to this girl. She made thoughts of Indigo disappear, and at that moment I wanted to kiss her…just to see what it was like. As soon as the thought reached my mind, Rena's lips were against mine, cold and wet. She kissed me first. With her eyes closed, she grabbed the back of my head. It felt as if I was having an out-of-body experience.

A few minutes later she broke free and splashed out of the water, headed for her beach towel. Lying on her back, she stared at the stars.

"You okay?" I asked.

"I'm fine."

We lay there, side by side on our beach towels, searching the dark sky—for what, I wasn't sure. Maybe we were searching for answers to why we were attracted to each other. I knew that was what I was searching for. It was clear that Rena had a boyfriend. And as for me, I still had Indigo Summer under my skin. And Rena was probably regretting the kiss that had obviously caused fireworks between us. Maybe driving down to the beach had been a bad idea after all.

"I better get home, Marcus. My mom will be looking for me soon. She gets off work at ten, and if I'm not home, she'll launch a search party." She stood and picked up her towel. Shook the sand away. "You ready?"

"Yeah, I'm ready." I shook sand from my towel, too. "Let's go."

Rena led the way along the dirt trail and back to the car. An old-school Notorious B.I.G. tune was on the radio, and I bounced my head to it. Rena didn't say much during the drive home, and I wondered what was on her mind. I wondered if she had seen the same sparks that I had just minutes earlier. Wondered what that kiss meant to her, if anything. Did it mean she had betrayed her boyfriend—the boyfriend she claimed she didn't have—and now was she feeling guilty about it? I needed to know.

"What's wrong?"

"Nothing's wrong."

"You're acting different now. We were having a good time, and then..."

"I'm cool, Marcus. It was just a kiss. Don't read too much into it."

"It didn't mean anything to me," I lied. "Besides, you got a boyfriend, anyway."

"Who told you that I had a boyfriend?"

"Nobody had to tell me. I saw him pick you up the other day."

"That was just Cedric." She acted nonchalant about it. "He's not my boyfriend."

"It sure looked that way...the way you greeted him with a kiss and all," I said, trying desperately not to sound jealous, even though I was. "I guess you go around kissing everybody like that, huh?"

"Whatever, Marcus." Her eyes were steady on the road. "Let's forget about tonight, okay?"

As if that were possible!

"Cool with me," I said, and stared out the window the whole way back up I-45.

Mom had fallen asleep, stretched out on the living room sofa, a stack of papers in her lap; she still had her reading glasses on. An episode of *Sex and the City* was on the television. I tiptoed toward her, tried removing her glasses without waking her up, but it didn't work. Her eyes instantly popped open.

"How was the beach, sweetie?"

"It was cool, Ma. What you doing? Watching your eyelids?"

"Just finishing up some work." She took off her glasses and looked at me. "What's wrong? You look funny."

"Nothing's wrong." I grabbed the remote control. "You watching this?"

"No, you can turn."

I started flipping through the channels. Stopped when I found VH1, where New York from the reality show *I Love New York* was kissing some dude and telling him how much she loved him. It was funny, because on the last episode I had watched, she'd been telling another dude the same thing.

"Ma, why are girls so weird? One minute you think they really like you, and the next minute they treat you like you did something wrong. It's hard to understand them."

"You'll probably never understand them completely, Marcus." She laughed. "That's just the way it is, baby."

"I don't think I want to understand, either." I headed for the kitchen. Grabbed an ice-cream sandwich from the freezer.

"Have you thought about what we talked about? You know—the possibility of you moving here... with me? I really want you to consider it, Marcus. The schools here are great, and I think you would do well."

"I'll think about it, Ma. I kinda like Atlanta, and all my friends are there."

"You can always make new friends, Marcus. You're outgoing. I know you won't have any problem meeting girls, with your cute self." She laughed. "You're not getting too serious with that young lady back in Atlanta...what's her name? Indigo."

Indigo Summer, the girl I used to think was the most beautiful girl in the world—that is, until I met Rena.

"No, I'm not getting too serious, Ma."

"That's good. Take it slow, baby. You're still young—got plenty of time for girls. Right now you need to focus on school, and your future."

"I know, Ma." I wanted to tell her that I wasn't a little kid anymore. That I'd grown to be a very responsible young man who had a Master Plan. But I decided not to. Instead, I flipped the channel to MTV and watched *Punk'd*. Before long, sleep found me right there on the sofa and I gave in to it.

chapter 9

Indigo

I checked out my booty in the dressing room mirror at Charlotte Russe, making sure the jeans fit just right. They were perfect, and I turned around and checked the front, stuck my hands down into the pockets. I slipped the top with spaghetti straps over my head to see if it looked right with the jeans. The outfit looked good on me, and I stepped outside the small dressing room to let Sabrina take a look.

"Brina, what you think about these jeans?"

She popped her head outside of her dressing room door, gave my jeans a scan. "Those are cute, Indi," she said. "Turn around, let me see the back."

I did a quick spin, sticking my behind out as I placed my hand on my hip.

"What about the top?" I asked her.

"Cute, but come here."

I walked over to the door of Sabrina's dressing room. She pulled on the bottom of my blouse in order to expose more cleavage. She straightened the spaghetti straps. "There, that's better. You gotta show the world what you got, girl. Even though you don't have that much." She laughed. "Wait until you have kids...then you'll have something to fill this little top out."

Sabrina checked out the back of her jeans in the mirror. "You like these, Indi?"

"They're cute."

"Yeah, I think I want them." She smiled and then slammed her door shut.

I stood in line behind Sabrina as she purchased a pair of silver hoop earrings and a pair of sunglasses with the large frames and pink lenses. After the salesperson rang up her purchase and handed Sabrina her change, I placed my jeans and blouse on the counter. I pulled a twenty-dollar bill out of my purse and handed it to the girl behind the counter, who had an Afrocentric hairstyle. She smiled when she handed me fifty-seven cents: my change, and the only money that I had to my name.

Daddy had promised to send me fifty dollars in the mail, but I had yet to receive it. So until he got around to it, I was officially broke. The jeans fit my body perfectly, so they were worth the sacrifice.

Sabrina and I tried on dresses that we found on the Macy's clearance rack, and shoes that were on sale at the Wild Pair. We stopped at Starbucks and ordered white chocolate mochas with a splash of vanilla in each. We sat in the comfortable chairs at Starbucks, listened to the eccentric music playing in the store and watched as people stepped up to the counter and ordered cappuccinos or other flavored coffees. We laughed at the big woman who ordered three pieces of chocolate cake and sat there and ate every crumb. We stepped into Victoria's Secret and smelled the new fragrances and lotions, and then ended our day at the mall with a quick breeze through the record store, in search of Chris Brown's new CD. Once we found it, Sabrina was eager to get to the car to play it. As she backed Dugan's Chevy out of the tight parking space, I ripped the plastic off the CD and popped it in.

"He is so fine," Sabrina said, then pulled a Newport out of her purse and lit it.

"Yes, he is," I said.

"Check this out, Indi." Sabrina reached into the

backseat for her huge Coach bag. The jeans that she'd tried on at Charlotte Russe were crumpled up inside her purse.

"The jeans you tried on! You stole them?"

"I had to have them. They were just so cute, I couldn't pass them up."

I looked out the window. Shoplifting was not something that I did, and I was nervous. I kept thinking that the cops would be looking for us soon.

"Oh, don't tell me you've never shoplifted before, Indi."

"Never," I said.

"Oh, I forgot, Uncle Harold buys you everything your little heart desires." She laughed. "You're a spoiled little rich girl."

The statement she made couldn't be further from the truth. My father wasn't rich, and he didn't buy me everything I wanted. I rarely got anything without working for it or begging for it. She had it all wrong. I didn't want her to think I was a "spoiled little rich girl," so I played along.

"That's cool that you got those jeans, girl. They were so cute on you!"

"You think so?" she asked.

"You should wear them tonight when we go out," I said.

"You know what? I probably will," Sabrina said, and then slowed at a stop sign.

We both rolled our windows all the way down and let the wind blow through our hair as we pulled out of the mall parking lot and into traffic. Chris Brown serenaded us as we breezed through the streets of Chi-town on a hot summer afternoon.

"You hungry?" Sabrina asked.

"A little bit," I told her.

"Cool. My girlfriend Trish is firing up the grill and she invited us over."

The tires of Dugan's car brushed against the curb as we pulled up in front of a ranch-style house with at least twenty people on the front porch. A Snoop Doggy Dogg track was being played—loud. Bottled beers were being turned up by some of the roughest-looking characters I'd ever seen in my life, and I was hesitant about stepping out of the car.

"Trish here?" Sabrina asked as she headed up the walkway.

"She in the house." A tall, slender man pointed toward the door and offered us something to drink. "Y'all want a beer?"

"No thanks," we said in unison, and stepped into the house.

People in the living room sat around on sofas and

talked loud enough to be heard over the music. Four people sat at the kitchen table playing dominoes. In the backyard, several others danced to the sounds of Snoop, while two guys flipped burgers on a barbecue grill.

"Sabrina, girl, what's up?" A short, dark girl with gold extensions in her hair walked toward us. Her long fingers were wrapped around a red plastic cup, and each long nail had a different design.

"Trish, what's good?" Sabrina asked her.

"It's all good." Trish smiled, and that was when I noticed the gold tooth in the front of her mouth. It was not attractive at all.

"That's what's up." My cousin gave Trish a tight squeeze. "This is my cousin Indigo. Indigo, meet Trish."

"Hi," I said.

"What's up, girl?" Trish smiled my way. "Y'all hungry?"

"Starving," Sabrina answered for both of us.

"Come on. The food's inside."

We followed Trish back into the kitchen, where she pulled a roasting pan filled with barbecued ribs and chicken out of the oven. She handed us a couple of paper plates and forks, and it wasn't long before both plates were overflowing with food. Trish poured us each a cup of Kool-Aid, and we stood around in the kitchen eating barbecue and watching as people slammed dominoes onto the table.

Before long, we were all in the middle of the floor doing the Cupid Shuffle. It was fun hanging out with Sabrina and her friends. My friends in Atlanta were nothing like this.

chapter 10

Marcus

The sound of knocking shook me out of my sleep, and I glanced over at the clock on my nightstand. Nine-thirty. I wiped sleep from my eyes and sat up on the side of the bed. I grabbed a T-shirt, pulled it over my head and headed for the door. Peeked through the peephole. Swung the door open.

"What's up with you knocking on my door at the crack of dawn every morning?" I asked Michelle.

"Marcus, it's way past dawn. It's almost ten o'clock," Michelle said. "Guess what?"

"What?"

"Guess," she insisted.

"Just tell me."

"I got tickets to see Lil Wayne on Friday night...at the Toyota Center!"

"Seriously?"

"Front-row seats and backstage passes, too," she said, and held the tickets in the air. "You wanna go?"

"No doubt." I snatched them from her, just to see if they were real.

They were real, all right. I handed them back.

"Cool, we can go, then," Michelle said, and stepped inside. She went straight for the kitchen. "Your mom didn't make us pancakes this morning?"

"She never made *us* pancakes in the first place. Those were my pancakes that you grubbed on the other day."

"That's okay, I'll just have a bowl of cereal." She giggled, and then pulled a bowl from the shelf. She looked in the pantry and found a box of Fruity Pebbles.

"Why don't you just make yourself at home?" I said sarcastically, and shook my head as Michelle did just that.

I made my way down the hallway and into the bathroom, washed my face and brushed my teeth. I went into my bedroom and grabbed my watch, slipped it onto my wrist. Glanced out the window at the pool. Rena was in her lifeguard uniform, sitting on her throne—her lifeguard chair. She put her whistle in her mouth, blew it and yelled at some kid. Her hair was pulled back into a ponytail. I watched her as she climbed down from the chair and went for a swim. I wanted to be next to her again and decided that I should go for a swim—just as soon as I got rid of Michelle.

She was already crunching on Fruity Pebbles and flipping through the channels on the television when I walked back into the room.

"This video is so hot!" Michelle said. "Check it out."

"Yeah, it is pretty hot."

It was a Plies video, featuring Akon—a video where sexy girls shook their hips in slow motion. It was one of the top videos on *106 & Park* that week, and one that was in my top ten.

I watched as Michelle bounced around in the middle of the floor. I was surprised that she had rhythm, and I began to wonder how she would look if she got rid of those pop-bottle glasses and actually invested in a pair of contacts. And what if she didn't wear braces and had straight, white teeth, and micro braids like the other girls I knew, instead of the silly ponytail that she wore on the back of her head? She seemed to be somewhat pretty on the inside. I just wondered what she would be like if she was pretty on the outside, too.

It was a hot summer day, and I couldn't wait to cool off in the pool. There was no hope of getting rid of Michelle as we both stepped out into the Texas heat. I had already spotted Rena from a distance, and watched as she paced the edge of the pool—back and forth—her whistle in her mouth, just waiting to be blown at someone violating the rules. I watched her, thinking of our kiss at the beach, and wondered if she'd thought of me when she got home. And wondering where her attitude had come from so suddenly that night. Had I done something wrong?

The tapping of a basketball shook me from my trance.

"What's up, Michelle? You're still as ugly as ever," said a short guy who favored Martin Lawrence, with his short cut, big teeth and big ears. He grinned at Michelle as he insulted her. He was wearing gray shorts that hung past his knees, and the number 23 on his Miami Heat jersey was beginning to peel. He dribbled the ball between his legs and pretended to shoot it into an imaginary basket.

"You are so stupid, Andre. You should grow up." Michelle rolled her eyes and sucked her teeth.

"You playing ball somewhere, man?" I asked. I didn't remember seeing a basketball court anywhere.

"Court right up the street, dog," Andre said. "You play?"

"Yeah, I play."

"Everybody plays up there. We can probably get the next game if we leave now."

I thought about it for a moment. I was just about to go for a swim and flirt with the sexy lifeguard at the pool. I wasn't even dressed for a game of basketball—I wore swimming trunks, and flip-flops on my feet.

"I was about to go for a swim," I said, and glanced back over at the pool. I wanted to go for a swim, but part of me wanted to shoot some hoops, too.

"Suit yourself, dog." Andre continued to bounce the ball, headed toward the subdivision entrance.

"Wait, man," I told him, "let me get my sneakers."

He nodded and agreed to wait for me. I took the stairs two at a time, changed shoes and ran back outside with a wifebeater on, and Jordans on my feet. I caught up with Andre. Michelle was close behind, as usual. She was quickly becoming my shadow.

"What position you play?" I asked Andre.

"Point guard," he boasted, "and let me tell you, I'm bad on the court...weaving in and out, in between the tall dudes. They can't touch me, dog."

"You that good, huh?" I asked.

"I can't even tell you in words. I gotta show you."

"Please," Michelle said, swinging her neck from side to side. "Boy, you can't play no ball."

"Shut up, girl, with those magnifying glasses on your face."

"You shut up, with your learning-disabled self," Michelle came back. "When you gon' stop riding the short bus and ride a regular bus like the rest of us?"

"Be quiet, girl," Andre said. "Hey, Marcus, like I was saying before I was rudely interrupted...my game is tight. Believe that."

Andre was talking a bunch of trash, and I wondered if he really did have game. The three of us jaywalked across a busy street, a tow truck coming very close to running us over. We cut through the parking lot of a Shell gas station, and then ended up on the backside of a Diamond Shamrock store. Across the street from the store was a playground where a tall dude was dunking a basketball into a rusty goal without a net. There were about ten dudes in the game and another twenty on the sideline awaiting their turns. I doubted that Andre or I would get a chance to play before dark, but I instantly felt a rush of excitement just to be able to watch the game being played.

A short, dark guy with a bald head took the ball out, passed it to his tall teammate with a nappy Afro, who dribbled it downcourt. Just as he went up for a layup, an opponent from the other team— a light-skinned dude with buckteeth—grabbed his shirt and prevented him from shooting.

"Foul!" Nappy Afro yelled.

"Hey, I didn't touch you, man," Bucktooth protested.

"Man, you grabbed my shirt." Nappy Afro was in Bucktooth's face in an instant.

Bucktooth pushed him, and before I knew it they were on the ground, rumbling. That is, until someone pulled them off each other.

"I quit," Nappy Afro said, and grabbed his shirt from the ground. He tossed it across his shoulder and headed off the court.

"We need a fill-in." A somewhat heavy dude with braids that needed to be redone scanned the crowd.

"I got next game." A guy standing next to the fence walked up. "I'll wait, though."

Heavy Dude looked into the bleachers. I must've stood out in the crowd, because he immediately zeroed in on me.

"Hey, man...you play?" he asked me.

"Yeah, I play."

"Come on, then," he said.

I stood and stepped down from the bleachers. Andre looked as if he'd been betrayed. I pulled my wifebeater over my head and tossed it to Michelle for safekeeping. Heavy Dude threw me the ball and told me to take it out. I stepped on the other side of the white line and passed the ball to a brown boy wearing sweatpants and raggedy sneakers. He caught it and headed down the court. When he got into trouble, he passed the ball to Heavy Dude, who handed it off to me as I split through the middle. I sank it into the basket with one swift move and headed downcourt. My teammates slapped me high fives before I took the ball out again.

Before long, we were only down by four points and I had six baskets under my belt. The court became more and more crowded, and by the time Brown Boy dunked the ball, we had managed to win the game. The losers were replaced by a different set of dudes and a new game began. A couple of hours later I glanced over at the bleachers at Andre and Michelle. They were still there, Andre hoping to get some play action, but he had been looked over all day. I felt his pain.

"Hey, man, I'm tired," I told Heavy Dude. "Why don't you let the little dude over there play?"

"Who, Andre?" Heavy Dude asked. "Man, he can't play no ball. Stick around a little longer, bro. We got this game wrapped up tight."

After the fifth game, I was exhausted and wanted nothing more than to get home, grab a turkey sandwich or some leftover tacos. I wanted a Cherry Coke so bad I could taste it.

"I'm done, man," I told Heavy Dude.

"Cool." He signaled to the others that it was time to quit. As we headed toward the bleachers, he asked, "What's your name, anyway, man?"

"Marcus." I held my fist out to give him some dap.

"I'ma call you Flash, because when you run down-court, you're like a flash of lightning, man." We gave each other dap. "Where'd you learn to play like that?"

"Been playing in leagues all my life. I play on the team at school, too."

"That's cool, bro. I'm Eldridge. But everybody just calls me El," he said. "You coming back tomorrow, Flash?"

"Yeah, I'll be here."

"Cool, I'll see you tomorrow then, man."

"No doubt."

Michelle and Andre stepped down from the bleachers.

"Can I have my shirt, please?"

"Marcus, you were so good." Michelle tossed the shirt my way. "You looked like a professional ballplayer—like Wade or Kobe."

"You do have game, dog," Andre said, and I was sure it took everything he had just to pay me a compliment, especially after he had bragged about his game.

We didn't discuss the fact that he didn't get any playing time. I didn't want to embarrass him any more than he already was. We just headed back the way we came—across the street to the Diamond Shamrock, and then back through the Shell parking lot. We jaywalked across the busy street again and strolled into the parking lot of our subdivision.

Rena was still seated on her throne as I passed by the pool. She looked my way, but I looked away this time. Headed up the stairs to our condo unit, unlocked the door and went straight for the shower.

When I stepped out of the shower, I knew Mom was home because there was old-school music playing and all sorts of spices were floating through the air. I could even hear voices and laughter over the music and wondered if she had company. I dried off and stepped out of the bathroom with a towel wrapped around my waist. I left the door cracked as I pulled on a pair of shorts and a T-shirt. That was when I heard a male voice and wondered who was in our home.

I stepped into the kitchen, where Mom was frying pork chops smothered in a mixture of New Orleans spices. She had a pair of tongs in one hand and a glass of wine in the other, shaking her hips to Marvin Gaye's "Distant Lover." The smell of a cigar suddenly assaulted my nose. I peeked into the living room to find a tall, thin black man in the middle of the floor, singing the words of the song and puffing on a cigar.

"You must be Marcus." He grinned and held his hand out.

"How you doing?" I asked, giving him a firm handshake. "Yes, I'm Marcus."

"This is my baby," Mom said as she appeared in the living room. "Marcus, this is Leon."

"Nice to meet you," I told Leon.

"Marcus, I understand you're considering a move here." Leon wore a pin-striped suit with perfectly shined shoes. The cuff links on the sleeves of his shirt were gold and sparkling as he took a drink from his shot glass.

"I'm thinking about it. But I haven't really made a decision yet."

"I know your mom would love to have you here. The three of us could really have a good life together."

The three of us? When did he become a part of this twosome?

"I've asked your mother to marry me." Leon smiled at Mom, who was holding her hand in the air and flashing the huge rock that he had placed on her finger. "And of course she said yes."

"When did all this happen?" I wanted to know.

"Over lunch this afternoon," Mom explained.

"What do you think about that, son?" Leon asked, and placed his hand on my shoulder. "I'm going to be your stepfather."

I couldn't believe my ears. Mom was engaged to some dude she hadn't even introduced me to before now. I felt betrayed. I knew she had a boyfriend, but I had no clue that they were halfway to the altar. I didn't even have an opportunity to size him up, make sure his intentions were good. I didn't know if he was a criminal in his previous life or if he had done jail time. I hadn't had a chance to get to know him at all, and here they were planning a wedding. I didn't know if he had kids, or if he even liked kids. He was dressed in a tailored suit with a silk shirt and expensive shoes, but I had no idea what Leon did for a living. My first time laying eyes on the guy and I'm knocked upside the head with the prospect that he might be my stepfather soon.

It was the same way with Pop when he met Gloria. I didn't have a say in the matter; I was just told that I would have a new stepmother. Nobody warned me that my life would be turned upside down and that I would lose my father to a gold digger. Our relationship as I knew it was suddenly different—no more basketball games at Philips Arena, and no more rolling through Buckhead on a Sunday afternoon in Pop's pickup truck. No more eating TV dinners in our underwear while watching SportsCenter in the den. All of that changed. Instead of it being just Pop and me, we were now a threesome. Here I was going through the same thing all over again.

"Congratulations, I guess...." That was all I could say.

I walked into the kitchen, grabbed a Little Debbie chocolate cupcake from the shelf and stuffed the whole thing into my mouth. I poured myself a glass of milk and sat at the bar.

"That's all you have to say, Marcus?" Mom asked.

"What else is there to say, Mom?" I asked. "You didn't give me an opportunity to have a say in the matter."

"Marcus, Leon and I have been dating for the past nine months. You weren't here during that time, but I've been very eager for you to meet him."

Not eager enough, I thought. I'd been in Houston for almost a month, and this was the first I'd heard of Leon.

"You asked me to move here with you, Mom, but I had no idea that you wanted me to move here with you and someone else. I thought it was just going to be me and you."

"Marcus, you'll be gone away to college in the next couple of years. Where does that leave me? Alone again?" she asked. "I want happiness, too, just like your father has with Gloria."

"It's no big deal, Mom. I'm happy for you," I

said, "but I think I've made my decision about moving here. One stepparent is enough for me...and I already have Gloria."

With that, I hopped from the bar stool and headed back to my room. Before I walked out, I could see that Mom's eyes were a little moist. I had hurt her feelings. But she'd hurt mine, too, just springing this dude and this whole marriage thing on me like that. She hadn't even given me an opportunity to get to know the guy. She'd simply said, "Hey, Marcus, this is Leon...and by the way, we're getting married. What do you think of that?" How selfish was that? I remembered talking to him on the phone once last Christmas, when he asked me what Santa had brought me. I had long stopped believing in Santa and knew then that he couldn't possibly have any kids my age. And if he didn't have teenage kids of his own, how could he relate to me?

I stretched my legs across my bed, placed the headphones of my iPod into my ears and listened to Young Jeezy. I was tired from shooting hoops all day, and before long, I had dozed off. When I woke up, an afghan had been thrown over me, the old-school music had stopped playing and the house was quiet. I tiptoed into the living room to see if Mom and Leon were still there.

Mom sat on the sofa in her pajamas, the remote control in her hand.

"Hey, Ma, you okay?" I asked.

"Hey, sleepyhead. You fell asleep before dinner was done." She looked over at me. Her eyes bloodshot, like she'd been crying. "I fixed you a plate, though. It's on the stove."

"I'm sorry about earlier, Mom. I was kind of rude."

"Yes, you were. But it's okay, Marcus."

"It's just that you caught me off guard with your engagement news. And I don't even know the dude."

"You were right, Marcus. I should've introduced you to Leon long ago, when we knew that we were serious about each other. We should've flown to Atlanta, so that you could have spent some time with him...gotten to know him months ago."

"I'm sorry that we live so far apart."

"That's not your fault, baby. It's mine," she said. "But I'm trying to fix that."

"I know, Mom...and I've been thinking about it. I do want to move here, and go to school here." I wasn't sure why I said that, but I did. Seeing her with tears in her eyes did something to my heart, and this was the only way I knew to fix it. I wanted to see my mother laughing and happy, not with bloodshot eyes. And if my moving to Houston made her happy, that was what I wanted. "I'll call Pop later and let him know."

"Are you serious, Marcus?"

"Yeah, I'm serious," I told her.

"We can have your father ship your things here. That way you won't even have to go back to Atlanta."

"What about my Jeep?"

"Oh, don't worry about that old thing." She smiled. "I was waiting to surprise you, but…I guess I could tell you now…." She stood, walked into the kitchen and refilled her wineglass. "The BMW outside…it's yours."

"For real?"

"Yes, for real." She grabbed the keys from the bar and threw them my way. "It's your car."

"What will you drive?" I asked.

"There's a cute little Mercedes that I've had my eye on for a long time," she said. "Leon bought it for me today. That was part of his proposal. He had it all wrapped up in a bow."

"Are you for real?" I asked thoughtfully. "What does he do for a living, anyway?"

"He's a lawyer…actually, a partner at his firm,"

she said. "You're gonna like him, Marcus. He's really a good man."

I didn't know if I would like Leon, but I liked the fact that I was the new owner of a convertible BMW with leather seats and a bumping system. Maybe living in Houston wouldn't be so bad after all. Actually, it was all good until I told Pop.

"Have you lost your mind, Marcus?" Pop was nearly screaming in my ear after I told him the news.

"I think I might like to live with Mom for a little while, Pop," I told him. "I've lived with you since eighth grade. Now I want to stay with Mom during my last couple of years. She deserves that."

"She deserves that? Are you kidding me, son?" He was hurt. "This is the woman who walked out on us—on you—because she was tired of being a wife and mother, leaving us to pick up the pieces and get our lives back on track. And we did it, Marcus, me and you, we did it. Did you forget about all that?"

"No, Pop, I didn't forget. But regardless, I have to forgive her."

"Well, Marcus. That is your mother, and you should forgive her. I just don't want to see you hurt again," he said, "so you think long and hard about this…and if your decision is to stay in Houston with your mother, then I guess I have to support that."

My pop had done his best to raise me. He taught me things that only a father could instill in his son, things like how to be a hard worker and to be a man of character. He taught me that you should treat people the way you wanted to be treated. He spent time with me and encouraged me to do my best in school. I understood his hesitation about me living with my mother. When Mom left, I had a hard time emotionally. I even went to therapy for a little while to get through the difficult time. It was Pop who talked to me through the nights until I finally fell asleep. It was Pop who had done all the work of raising me through the difficult times, and now Mom wanted to come in and benefit from my most important years—the last two years of high school.

"Thanks, Pop." I needed his blessing. His opinion mattered to me. "I need your support in this."

"What kinda car did she buy you?"

"How do you know she bought me a car?"

"I know Dorothy Carter better than anyone else. She gets what she wants by any means necessary." Pop laughed sarcastically.

"She gave me a BMW."

"I knew it!"

"It doesn't mean that much to me, Pop. You know I'm not into material things. But it is nice. It's got the little sporty wheels on it and everything."

"Your Jeep is a good-running vehicle, Marcus," he said, "not to mention you saved up for months just to buy it with your hard-earned cash. That should mean something to you."

"It does, Pop. I love my Jeep," I said.

He was right. I had saved up for months just to buy my Jeep, and every week I washed it, waxed it and rubbed Armor All on the wheels to make them shine. I kept the interior spotless and had just put a hot system into it, with new speakers. My Jeep was my pride and joy.

"Your Jeep will be here waiting for you when you come for visits," he said. "And what about Indigo? What are you gonna do about her?"

"We broke up at the beginning of the summer. Made this stupid pact to be free to see other people," I told him. "It was her idea."

"You miss her?"

"Nah, Pop. I don't miss her one bit," I lied. Truthfully, I thought of Indigo every day. I missed everything about her, but I couldn't admit that to anyone. "There are plenty of honeys here. It's a single man's playground."

That was a phrase that I'd heard my pop use with his buddies before, "a single man's playground." I had been waiting for the perfect opportunity to use it, and it actually sounded pretty good—if I believed it. The girls in Houston really didn't mean anything to me. Rena was beautiful and all, but I didn't have any feelings for her. Not like I had for Indigo. Rena was just nice to look at. I'd originally had plans of reuniting with Indigo at the end of the summer when we both returned to Atlanta, but things had suddenly changed. I wouldn't be returning to Atlanta after all. The thought made me sad, but I couldn't let it get me down. I snapped out of it.

"What do you know about a single man's playground? Boy, you are something else." He laughed.

"I know, Pop, I'm just like you."

"Marcus, if living with your mother is what you really want, then you have my blessing. Just know that you always have a home in Atlanta if you change your mind. And I'm always here for you, son, anytime, day or night," Pop said. "You got that?"

"Yes, sir."

"Now tell your mama I said hello. I gotta go cut Mrs. Jackson's grass. Wish you were here to cut it for me."

"Pop, you could always hire somebody to cut it."

"Not a chance. I just put a new spark plug in that old lawn mower, and it's as good as new."

My father bought, sold and managed old properties for a living. Not only was he a landlord, but he was also the Mr. Fix-It Man and did all the repairs himself. He even cut the lawns of his elderly tenants. He refused to hire someone to do the work and didn't have any problem dragging me along to help him out. I hated the thought of unclogging toilets and trimming bushes, but I did it. And now that I was gone, Pop would have to do these things all by himself. Maybe he would finally see that he needed to get some help.

"Okay, Pop. I love you, man."

"Love you, too, Marcus," he said. "Be a good boy."

Before then, I wasn't sure about my decision to stay in Houston. I guess I was hesitant because I didn't want to hurt Pop. But after he gave me his blessing, I felt better about my decision. It was as if he had released me and I was free to make my mother happy for a while. I loved Pop for that; it proved just how unselfish he was, and I was glad that he was my father. The values he instilled in me were the same values that he claimed as his own. He practiced what he preached. My pop was a man of character, and I wanted to be just like him when I grew up.

chapter 11

Indigo

Nana and I strolled down the Magnificent Mile, sunshine beaming down on our foreheads. We popped our heads into Filene's Basement to look around a bit, and then stepped into Macy's so that Nana could pick up a pair of panty hose for church on Sunday. Nana bought me a pair of sandals and a purse at Payless. And then we dropped into Barnes & Noble. We stopped at Gino's for a pan of Chicago's deep-dish pizza. At Gino's the walls and tables were covered with graffiti. Everyone who ate there, no matter where they were from, left their names carved into the wooden tables and on the wall. There were so many names that I couldn't even read them all. Nana and I sat at a table near the window, and I sipped an ice-cold root beer while we waited for our pizza.

"So how did you enjoy your little outing the other night with Sabrina? Did you girls have a good time at the teen club she took you to?"

"Yes, ma'am."

Teen club? Sabrina had obviously made Nana believe that we were going to a teen club instead of the adult one we actually went to. I didn't like lying to Nana, and so to avoid the conversation, I changed the subject.

"You think we can take some pizza home for Uncle Keith, Nana?"

"Child, Uncle Keith is a grown man and can take care of himself." She chuckled. "I don't know, maybe we will take him a slice or two—if there's any left."

"You think he'll ever find his own place and move out?"

"I can only hope, sweet pea. Don't look like it's going to be anytime soon, though."

"I kinda like the thought of him being there with you...so you don't have to be alone."

"I don't mind being alone. I've been alone since the day your grandpa passed away."

"Do you get scared in the middle of the night sometimes...I mean in that big old house and all?"

"Child, I have lived in that house since your daddy was ten years old. I know every little nook and cranny, and I recognize all the noises. There is nothing in that house that makes me afraid," she said. "Now back to your little night out with Sabrina. I noticed you tried to avoid talking about it."

"I wasn't trying to—"

"Let me tell you something. I love Sabrina to death. I changed her diapers when she was a baby, just like I changed yours. But I don't necessarily approve of that little lifestyle she got going on over there. Now, she asked me if you could hang out with her the other night, and I want you to have a good time while you're here, but you won't be hanging out with her that often. You understand?"

"Yes, ma'am."

"It's not cute to have a two-year-old child at seventeen. Although I know we all make mistakes. But don't you go getting all glassy-eyed over somebody else's life."

"But, I didn't say anything about—"

"You didn't have to say anything, missy. I know you better than you know yourself," Nana said. "You make sure you stay in school and make good grades…and, Indi, continue to make good choices. You hear me?"

"Yes, ma'am."

"That's all I'm gonna say about it."

It was as if Nana had read my mind, because I did think that Sabrina had the perfect life. Even though she had made a mistake by getting pregnant and had disappointed her parents, she still had it going on, in my opinion. At seventeen she had her own apartment and could come and go as she pleased. She hung out with the big people in Chicago and had an older boyfriend—a hot older boyfriend. I'd have said she had more right in her favor than wrong.

When the waitress placed our piping-hot pizza in the center of the table, it was still sizzling. I didn't waste any time digging a slice out and placing it on my plate. Nana did the same, and we ate until we both were too stuffed to walk another block. Not to mention it had started pouring rain. I pulled my cell phone out and tried to reach Uncle Keith so he could pick us up, but he was nowhere to be found. At the curb, Nana hailed us a Yellow Cab, and we hopped into the backseat and headed home. As the rain trickled down the windshield of the cab, I thought about Sabrina and wondered how I could make my life turn out just like hers.

chapter 12

Marcus

The restaurant was decorated in bright yellow, red and orange. Spanish music played softly in the background, and Mexican spices were in the air. My stomach growled as I checked out what some of the other patrons were eating: tacos, enchiladas, burritos. Chips were being dipped into salsa, and wineglasses were being turned up by some of the ladies in the place. There was laughter in the air as we stood there waiting to be seated.

"*Hola*, Leon!" A beautiful Hispanic woman approached, wearing very provocative clothing and bouncing her hips way too hard.

"*Hola*, Marianna. *¿Cómo está?*" Leon started speaking Spanish very fluently, and I was in awe.

I remembered taking Spanish when I was in the eighth grade. I'd just barely passed with a low C. Spanish was not a class that interested me, and the teacher I'd had, Ms. Callahan, wasn't a very good one in my opinion. Each day she loaded us down with homework assignments and projects that I didn't understand, and she never even attempted to make the class interesting. Even though Ms. Callahan explained that it was essential that we learn a second language, I swore that I would never need Spanish again in life. But now I wanted to know what they were saying.

"Estoy bien, Leon. ¿Y usted?" the woman responded, telling Leon that she was doing fine. She asked how he was doing.

"Estoy bien," Leon responded.

As southwestern-style music continued to drift throughout the place, the Hispanic woman, who had round hips and large breasts, escorted us to a table near the window. Her face was a pretty vanilla color, and she had long, black, curly hair pulled back into a ponytail. Her smile brightened the room, and deep dimples danced across her round cheeks. I could've sworn that she was flirting with Leon or he was flirting with her as I slid into the booth and opened my menu. I took a peek over the top of the menu and caught Leon giving Marianna a glance that made me want to pull my cell phone out and take a picture so that I could show my mother.

"This is Marcus," Leon said to Marianna.

"Very nice to meet you, Marcus," Marianna said in her broken English. "You're a very handsome young man."

"Thank you," I said to her, trying my best not to blush. I couldn't help it.

"What can I get you to drink, Marcus?" I just knew my face had turned beet red as Marianna flashed her award-winning smile my way. She was beautiful, and she made me nervous.

"I'll just have a Cherry Coke," I told her.

"I'm sorry, but we don't have Cherry Coke." She smiled. "I can bring you a Coke and add a cherry. How 'bout that?"

I was mesmerized, and smiled back. "That's cool."

I didn't even drink regular Coke, but here I was ordering one. And when Marianna disappeared, I couldn't help wishing she would return soon, just so I could look at her.

"Snap out of it." Leon laughed, and I wondered how long he'd been watching me watch her. "Beautiful, isn't she?"

"She's all right," I lied, and then hid my face behind the menu.

Browsing through the menu, I decided on a combination meal that included tacos, enchiladas and a chicken burrito. I had a huge appetite, and since Leon was paying, I didn't mind ordering exactly what I wanted. I needed to check him out, anyway, see if he was the guy my mother thought he was. She kept raving about how wonderful Leon was...Leon this and Leon that. I needed to check him out for myself. It was her idea that we get together and get to know each other, but I was all for it. And what better way to do that than to hit him in his pockets, see if he was cheap. I wanted to feel him out, see if his intentions were good or if he was just a playboy out to stomp on my mother's heart. I wasn't having that, and I wanted him to know that up front.

"So, Leon, do you have any kids?" I asked the question that had been burning in my mind since I first met him.

"I have a daughter, Marcus. She's about your age," he said as he perused the menu. "Her name is Jasmine, and she lives in Maryland with her mother."

"Why doesn't she live in Texas with you?"

"Well, it doesn't really work like that. Her mother wanted to have custody of her. She's really better off living with her mother. Girls need that motherly love, you know what I mean?" he asked. "It's just like you, living with your father. It's always good for a young man to grow up around his father. Right?"

"I guess," I said, a million other questions zooming around in my head as Marianna brought our drinks.

My eyes took in all of her as she placed my Coke with the cherry in it on the table. When she smiled my way, I began to blush again. Marianna had a strange effect on men, and I could tell that Leon felt it, too. It was as if the two of us were frozen in time as she took our orders. She disappeared, and I was glad because I needed to regain my composure before I lost all my cool points in front of the man I was supposed to be investigating.

"Why do you live here instead of Maryland?" I asked. "What brought you to Texas?"

"I came here to work for a law firm that made me a great offer, one that I couldn't refuse."

"So you chose your career over being near your daughter?" I asked. "You sold out, huh?"

"I didn't sell out. I made a career choice that was best for both of us…my daughter and me. The more money I make, the better off Jasmine is."

"Even if it means you can't see her that often?"

"It's really not that serious, Marcus," Leon said. "I see Jasmine during the Christmas holidays and on spring break, and that's plenty for us."

"Why did you break up with her mother?" I asked. I knew I was being nosy, but these were important questions that needed a response.

"Well, Jasmine's mother and I were divorced five years ago. She decided that my long hours did not work for her any longer. She accused me of being a workaholic," he said. "That's what I like about your mother. She's a hard worker, too, and doesn't mind my long hours."

I guess he had a point. Mom was definitely a workaholic. But in my opinion she needed someone to help her relax, not someone who was just like her. I sat there across the table from Leon trying to determine what it was that my mother saw in him. He was a normal-looking man—he wasn't Denzel or anybody. It wasn't his looks that attracted her to him, that was for sure. He was skinny, and didn't appear to be someone who spent much time at the gym. He had money, but so did Mom. She was very successful and could buy just about anything she wanted. I had decided that Leon was a guy of mystery and it was up to me to crack the code.

"Did your daughter have to go through therapy over your divorce?"

"No. Over time, she was okay," he said.

"Well, I had to go to therapy when my parents got a divorce. My grades dropped and everything."

"But you snapped out of it eventually?"

"Eventually, yeah."

"The important thing is, your parents are happier apart than they probably ever were together. I don't believe that people should stay in unhealthy relationships just for the heck of it. Everybody loses in that situation."

I didn't comment. I still believed that my parents could've made it work if they'd really wanted to. I think they gave up hope.

"You play ball?" I asked, changing the subject.

"I can play a little bit." He smiled. "You wanna hit the courts later?"

"Yeah, that would be cool."

I wondered if Leon could shoot hoops and couldn't wait to get him out there on the court to find out. After dinner, we ended up at a local YMCA. In the locker room, Leon tossed me a pair of his old shorts and a T-shirt. Both of us changed quickly and rushed out onto the shiny buffed floor, where guys twice my age ran up and down the court. Some of them had bellies like Pop's that hung over the elastic in their shorts. Leon's legs were ashy and the size of light poles, and his shorts hung just past his knees. He ran out onto the court and joined his middle-aged buddies as they started running around and doing fancy moves like the Harlem Globetrotters.

One of them yelled my way, "Hey, young blood, come on out here and get this whipping, boy."

He obviously didn't know that I was Rufus Carter's boy, the kid who'd played in every league there was since the time he was five years old. The one who could run rings around the best of them on a basketball court. The starting forward for his school's basketball team. My right-hand layup was the prettiest in the entire Atlanta metro area, and they didn't even know it. I doubted that any of these old guys could whip me, but it would be fun watching them try. I jogged out onto the court, and someone immediately tossed me the ball.

"Take it out, boy," the man said, and I did as I was told.

I took the ball out and threw it to him. He dribbled down court, his belly bouncing with every movement. He and the other older men started passing it around to each other, tossing the ball behind their backs and dribbling between their legs. When it finally reached the last person, he tossed it into the basket with one hand, the ball rolling off his fingertips. To my surprise, these old guys were good, each displaying their own fancy jump shot. Even Leon could handle the ball like a pro, and I wondered if he had played on the team when he was in high school or college. I was worn-out by the time the game was over.

The car reeked with perspiration and funk as Leon and I headed home in his Lincoln Navigator.

"So did you have a good time, Marcus?" he asked.

I couldn't lie. I did have a good time. I had to admit, I had misjudged the old men on the court. I had misjudged Leon. I was so busy trying to find things that might be wrong with him that I forgot to find something right. I wasn't sure if he would make a good husband for my mother, but one thing I knew—he could shoot some hoops.

chapter 13

Marcus

I splashed into the water feetfirst and then came back up for a breather. Michelle jumped in behind me. Andre turned a flip into the pool and landed just a few feet away from me. The girl from the other day—the one wearing the yellow bikini—tossed a beach ball into the water and then dove in after it. She ended up just inches from my legs.

"Hi. Wanna play catch?" she asked.

"I do!" Andre answered, even though she wasn't talking to him.

Her eyes were focused on me.

"I'm Tiffany," she said, and then tossed me the ball.

"I'm Andre." He swam over and shook her hand.

"Nice to meet you, Andre," Tiffany said, and then looked at me. "What's your name?"

"I'm Marcus." I laughed at Andre. I would have to teach that boy how to keep his cool points, because he was losing them so fast, he was almost out of them. "And this is Michelle."

"Nice to meet you, Tiffany. You're new around here," Michelle said.

"I just moved here from San Diego. My dad's job transferred us, and so here I am. We live in Building C."

"I live in that building right there," Michelle said, and pointed at our building.

"I don't live in this subdivision," Andre said. "I live a few blocks away. I just come over here to swim in the pool."

"That's nice," Tiffany said. "So, Marcus, you live here?"

"Yes, I just moved here from Atlanta," I said. "I live in the same building as Michelle."

"So you're staying, Marcus?" Michelle asked, a grin on her face.

"Yeah, I think I might."

"You didn't tell me." Michelle splashed water in my face.

"I didn't know I was supposed to." I splashed water in her face.

Before I knew it, we were all splashing water at each other, having ourselves a nice little water fight. I laughed harder than I had in a long time after I dunked Michelle's head underwater. She threw water at me in retaliation. Tiffany jumped on my back and tried to dunk me, but she didn't have enough strength. Instead, I put her in a choke hold and dunked her. When she came back up, she splashed me and I ducked. Instead of hitting me, the water splashed across Andre's face, and he grabbed Tiffany's legs and pulled her under. We were all laughing and having fun. I barely heard the screech of the whistle and almost didn't see Rena standing at the edge of the pool with her hands on her hips and a frown on her face.

"No horseplay in the pool," she said. "Either cut it out or I'll have to ask you all to get out."

Everyone stared quietly at her. After she walked away, we all busted out laughing. I grabbed the beach ball and tossed it at Tiffany. She caught it and then tossed it to Andre. Andre tossed the red, white and blue ball to Michelle, and we continued like that until we got bored. Horseplay, as Rena put it, was so much more fun.

"Let's go to my house and watch DVDs," Tiffany finally said. "Maybe we can even order a pizza."

"What kind of DVDs you got?" I asked.

"I have everything you can think of. All of Tyler Perry's movies, including a bootleg copy of *Why Did I Get Married?*"

"That movie was so good," Michelle said. "I saw it twice at the theater."

"It was pretty good," Andre said, "but what kind of action-packed stuff do you have?"

"I have a few Bruce Willis action flicks. Most of them are old, though."

"That's cool," I said. "I can get down with some pizza."

"How much does something like that cost...pizza, I mean?" Andre asked, and dug deep into the pockets of his trunks, as if he actually had some cash there. "Because I have like...zero dollars."

"It's okay, I have my dad's credit card," Tiffany said, and pulled herself out of the water. "Let's go."

Tiffany's house was decorated in cream-colored furniture with black accessories. Expensive art hung on every wall, and the carpet was as white as snow.

"Take your shoes off and leave them in the foyer," she said. "I'll get the movies."

She disappeared into one of the back bedrooms while Andre, Michelle and I took a seat on the living room floor, a towel underneath our bottoms. We were all still soaking wet from the pool and didn't want to soil the furniture. Tiffany handed me a stack of movies and then started punching in numbers on the cordless phone. She ordered two pizzas and a bottle of Pepsi.

I started flipping through the stack of movies and passing them on to Andre.

"Let's watch this." Michelle held an old movie, *Friday,* in the air.

"Yeah, let's watch that," Andre said. "Even though I've seen it a million times, it just gets better and better."

Tiffany slipped the movie into the DVD player, and we all laughed our hearts out until the pizza man finally tapped on the door. I grabbed two slices of pepperoni and slapped them onto my plate. I filled my glass with Pepsi, even though I was a die-hard Coke man. Andre had finished three slices of cheese pizza before I even had a chance to bite into my first one. Tiffany and Michelle each started off with one slice, and before long, Andre and I had finished off the pepperoni.

Several hours later, the four of us were old

friends, laughing at movies that we'd all seen a million times each. We'd finished watching *Friday* and *Next Friday* by early afternoon.

"Anybody up for *Friday After Next*?" Tiffany asked after the credits from the previous movie had rolled up the screen.

"I gotta get home," Michelle said, and stood. She slipped her flip-flops back onto her feet. "I gotta clean up the house before my mom gets there."

"I better get going, too." I stood. "Andre, you coming?"

"Nah, man, I'm gonna stay here and check out *Friday After Next*," he said.

Tiffany didn't seem to mind that Andre was the only one staying, and I couldn't help laughing inside as I slipped my flip-flops on. I followed Michelle down the wooden steps and across the parking lot. As we passed the pool area, I noticed that it was still crowded. Lots of girls in bathing suits bouncing around in the water. Rena was no longer on her throne; in her place was a redheaded white guy with freckles all over his face.

When I stepped into the breezeway of our condo unit, I was surprised at what I saw. Rena was sitting on the stairs, her hands clasped beneath her chin.

Michelle and I both stopped in our tracks at the sight of her.

"Hey, Marcus," Rena said.

"Rena, what's up? What are you doing out here?"

"Waiting for you."

I didn't know what to say. Both Rena and Michelle stared at me, waiting for my response. I didn't have one. I didn't know what was going on in this girl's head.

"Hey, I'll catch you later, Michelle," I said, trying to dismiss her.

Michelle hesitated for a moment, as if she was waiting to hear the conversation between Rena and me. I gave her a look that said "You can go now." She sucked her teeth, rolled her eyes at Rena and then tramped on up the stairs.

"You want to walk over to McDonald's later for ice cream, Marcus?" Michelle hollered back down the stairs.

"Yeah, that's cool. Just come and get me when you're ready."

"I'll be done cleaning up in about an hour," she said, and then unlocked the door of her unit.

"What's up with you and Nerdy Girl?" Rena asked.

"She's my friend," I said. "What's up with you?"

"I've been waiting for you all afternoon, Marcus," she said. "Did you enjoy spending the entire afternoon with little Miss Yellow Bikini?"

She was jealous. That explained why she was camped out at the bottom of my stairs. I laughed, stepped over her and went up the stairs. She sat there and watched me as I stuck my key in the door.

"You coming?"

She stood and walked slowly up the stairs and into my house. Just as I was shutting the door, Michelle stuck her head out of her door, shook it from side to side with her lips pursed. "McDonald's... ice cream...in an hour." She sighed and then slammed her door. I shut my door and locked it behind me. Rena stood in the middle of the foyer, waiting for me to tell her where to go.

"You wanna watch some TV?" I asked.

"Can I have something to drink, Marcus?"

"Yeah, okay. You want Cherry Coke or bottled water?"

"I'll take some Cherry Coke."

I pulled the two-liter bottle out of the refrigerator, grabbed two cups from the cabinet. I poured a cup of Cherry Coke for Rena and passed it to her. She grabbed it and started looking around the house, checking things out.

"Your mother is a good decorator, Marcus. The house is very pretty."

She walked into the hallway and observed the photos on the wall. There were several of me—one of them was my second-grade photo and my two front teeth were missing. Another was my sixth-grade photo and I was sporting a lopsided Afro. Rena talked about how cute I was in the second-grade photo and then turned to me.

"What was up with your hair in this picture, Marcus?" she asked, pointing to my sixth-grade photo with the nappy Afro.

"What you mean? I was cute then, too."

"If you say so." Rena started laughing and I had to laugh, too.

She made her way all the way down the hall and took a peek into my mother's bedroom.

"My mom's room," I said.

"Where's your room?" she asked.

I nodded toward the room across the hall. She peeked into the bedroom and then went inside, plopped down on my bed.

"You comfy?" I asked as she made herself at home.

"Yes, I am, Marcus Carter." She leaned back on my bed. "What's your middle name?"

"Frederick Henry."

"Is it Frederick or Henry?" Rena giggled.

"It's both...Frederick and Henry." I laughed. "My name is Marcus Frederick Henry Carter. Marcus, named after Marcus Garvey. Frederick, named after Frederick Douglass, who fought to end slavery. And Henry was my great-grandfather's name on my father's side of the family. Anything else?"

"Nope, nothing else." She smiled.

I plopped down on the bed beside her. I brushed her hair out of her face and caressed her cheek.

"So you were jealous of Tiffany, huh?"

"What? No, I wasn't jealous," she said.

"What do you call it, then? I come home and see you posted up on my steps. What was that about?"

"Okay, maybe I was just a little jealous," she said. "I like you, Marcus."

"I like you, too," I told her, "but what happened the other night at the beach? Why you start tripping like that after we kissed?"

"I guess I didn't know I was so attracted to you...until that moment, Marcus. It scared me a little bit."

"You don't have to be scared with me, Rena. I won't hurt you."

She was beautiful, and my heart started to pound as she ran her hand across my waves. Pretty soon, her lips were against mine again, just like they were when we were at the beach. I wanted to pull away, didn't want to feel uncomfortable again. It had been a long, quiet drive from the beach that night, and I still wasn't sure what had gone wrong. I wanted to pull her arms from around my neck, but they seemed to belong there as her tongue made circles inside my mouth. I gently laid her back onto the bed and was on top of her in an instant, both of us breathing heavily.

I pulled her lifeguard T-shirt over her head, and she didn't fight it. In fact, she helped me take it off, and soon she was lying there in her bikini top, chill bumps up and down her arm. I unzipped her khaki shorts and pushed my hand down into them. I helped her out of them as they dropped to the floor. I hopped up and shut the blinds. As I pulled my wallet from my top drawer in search of a condom, I took a glance at the beautiful girl stretched out across my bed wearing nothing more than a sexy bikini. I was in the zone. My hormones were out of control as I continued to search for the one condom that I kept in my wallet at all times in case of emergencies like this one.

"Big Things Poppin'," the ring tone on my cell phone, interrupted my flow. It was a ring tone that Indigo had insisted on, since she was in love with T.I. At one time, I thought I was going to have to hunt him down and mess him up because she talked about him so much. He was her favorite artist. Out of habit, I grabbed my cell phone out of the pocket of my jeans and looked at the screen.

Speak of the devil, I thought as I stared at Indigo's name on the screen. Why was she calling? And why now? Was she psychic or something? Before I could think it through, I hit the green button to answer the call.

"Hello," I said, but nobody responded. "Hello... anybody there?"

She was gone, and so was my mood. I glanced over at Rena, who was patiently waiting for my return.

"Marcus?" My mother was in the house, and my heart started to beat at an uneven pace. "Marcus, are you home, baby?"

"Is that your mother?" Rena asked, and immediately started putting her shorts and T-shirt back on.

I decided to head Mom off at the pass; didn't want her busting in on us. I stepped out of the room and pulled the door shut behind me. Mom was in the kitchen, putting groceries up.

"What you doing, baby?"

"Nothing," I said. "Let me help you with that. Why don't you go on in your room and change into some sweats or something? You want me to start dinner?"

I started placing canned goods on the shelf and the milk and eggs into the refrigerator.

"No, Marcus, I can start dinner."

"Okay, cool. I like your dinner better, anyway." I laughed way too hard at my own comment. "But go on and get changed into something more comfortable before you start. I'll put the groceries away."

Mom looked at me sideways but did as I said and headed for her bedroom. I hoped that Rena had enough sense to stay in my room until I came back for her. Once Mom had stepped into her room and shut the door, I bolted for my bedroom.

"I'm sorry, but you gotta get out of here," I whispered to Rena.

"I know," she agreed, and followed me as we tiptoed down the hallway.

"Marcus, I was thinking…" Mom stepped out of her room and was startled to see Rena and me in the hallway. We were almost there. "Marcus, who is this?"

"Oh, Ma, this is, uh…this is…"

"Rena." She helped me out, because I was at a loss for words. "I'm Rena, Mrs. Carter."

"Well, it's very nice to meet you, Rena." Mom shook Rena's hand. "I didn't know that Marcus had company. Are you staying for dinner?"

"I would love to," Rena said before I could protest, and then followed my mother into the kitchen.

"Good, then you can help." Mom smiled.

"I would love to help." Rena was enjoying this.

"Why don't you grab the olive oil from the shelf, pour a little into this frying pan and start sautéing the onions and bell peppers," Mom told Rena. "I'll be right back. I'm going to change clothes. Marcus, can I see you for a minute?"

I followed Mom into her bedroom and she pulled a pair of sweatpants out of a drawer.

"Marcus, I don't mind you having company. You're a responsible young man, and I'd like to think that you're making good choices. But I don't think it's appropriate for a young lady to be in your bedroom," she said, and pulled an old T-shirt from another drawer. "If you're going to entertain company, you can do so in the living room. Do I make myself clear?"

"Yes, ma'am. It won't happen again."

"Good, then we won't have to go here again," she said. "Now go and help that girl sauté the veggies. I don't even know if she can cook."

"Okay, Ma. Sorry."

I stepped out of the room and shut the door behind me. Went into the kitchen to help Rena sauté the vegetables; found myself chopping an onion for the first time in my life.

"Was she mad?" Rena whispered.

"No. She was cool."

"Are you disappointed that we didn't go all the way, Marcus?"

"Nah, it's cool. Guess it wasn't the right time."

"Guess not," Rena said, "but I like you a lot. And if I ever give it up, I want it to be with you."

"Are you a virgin?"

"Of course," she said, and then started stirring the bell pepper around in the pan.

I dumped the onions that I had chopped into the pan, and she stirred those around too. I was glad that Rena and I had been interrupted. There was no telling what would've happened if we'd still been in that room. I never wanted to be responsible for stealing someone's virginity, especially when I didn't love her. And she wasn't even my girl. Taking a girl's virginity was a huge decision, and not one to be made lightly. Until I got to know Rena better, I would not be the dude to change her life—not in that manner. And I didn't think she should be so careless about it. I wasn't ready for that type of change, and neither was she.

I couldn't wait for dinner to be over and for Rena to leave. I wanted to call Indigo back and find out why she had called. I wondered if she was missing me like I was missing her. I wanted to know if she'd met someone new, and if she still had hopes of hooking up with me at the end of the summer. Even though I wouldn't be returning to Atlanta, I wondered if she longed for this stupid pact to be over.

chapter 14

Indigo

Nana had insisted on calling Marcus to find out if he was enjoying his summer vacation in Houston. I hoped he didn't think it was me calling, or worse, think that I was stalking him or something. I had to admit, I did miss Marcus, but I couldn't let him know that. If I admitted to missing him, then I'd have to admit that I'd been wrong—wrong to suggest a pact that was stupid to begin with. But I would never do that. Instead, I needed to meet a guy who would make the whole thing worth it.

Marcus and I had taken a photo at one of those booths at the mall. It was a black-and-white photo, and in the picture Marcus was holding up rabbit ears behind my head. I slept with that picture underneath my pillow every night and took a glance at it every chance I got. Didn't want to forget what he looked like over the summer. I still remembered the way he laughed and the way he said my name. I could even hear his voice in my head sometimes.

I had been in Chicago for three solid weeks and hadn't once bumped into Jordan Fisher, the boy who had been my summer boyfriend since I was seven years old. I wondered whether he still lived on Nana's block, because I hadn't seen his face in the neighborhood. One day when I went for a walk to the gas station to get a package of Skittles, I almost stepped up to his door, but I changed my mind. I did bump into his best friend, Lance Cooper, when I stopped at the end of the block and watched the neighborhood boys play a game of basketball.

"Indi, what you doing here?" Lance asked.

"Staying at my grandmother's for the summer."

"You still as fine as you wanna be." Lance smiled.

"Where's Jordan? Does he still live in that brick house on the corner?"

"Yeah, he lives there. I'm surprised he's not out here shooting hoops," Lance said. "Why? You still like him?"

"I was just curious. Wondered how he was doing."

"Why don't you go knock on the door? He's probably in there."

"I'll pass," I told Lance, and then headed back down the block toward Nana's. "I'll see you later."

"I'll tell Jordan that you were looking for him."

"Whatever, Lance."

Nana and I had settled into the den, sharing a bowl of Orville Redenbacher's popcorn and watching the *American Idol Rewind. American Idol* had been our favorite show since the first time it came on television, and we laughed so hard at the auditions. It was hard to believe that people actually went on national TV and behaved the way some of the *American Idol* wannabes did. Only a handful of them actually had nice singing voices, though some of them were convinced that they were the next great star, but couldn't hold a note to save their souls.

Our next favorite show was *Deal or No Deal*. When I was in Atlanta, Nana and I would call each other on the phone during the show.

"Deal or no deal, Indi?" Nana would ask, just as some contestant was trying to decide what to do.

"I say no deal, Nana." I was the risk taker between the two of us; Nana was the conservative one. She'd yell at the person on TV and tell them to take the deal that the banker was offering. And she'd call them all kinds of stupid when they didn't. I often wondered what it would be like if Nana and I had a chance to join Howie Mandel on that stage as contestants. If I were a contestant, Nana would be on the edge of her seat, screaming for me to take the deal, and I'd be trying to convince her that I could win the million dollars.

"Indi, if you don't take that deal, I'm going to whip your behind." I could just hear Nana saying that.

It would be the one time I'd have to take that whipping, because if I believed that I had a million dollars in the briefcase, I would not take the deal.

We laughed as Simon told some girl that her voice was horrendous. Simon had such a way with words and showed no mercy when telling people how bad they were. I felt bad for some of them. Paula always said whatever Randy said, and Nana and I swore up and down that Simon and Paula had a thing going on during one season. We shook our heads every time Paula opened her mouth. After she would give her little spiel to the contestants, Nana and I would look at each other and say, "What?" in unison. Paula always seemed to be in her own little world.

When my cell phone rang, I snatched it up...wondered if it was Marcus. When Jade's name flashed across the screen, I decided not to answer. I'd call her back later.

"You're not going to answer?" Nana asked, that skeptical look on her face.

"It's Jade. I'll call her back when *American Idol* goes off."

"Afraid it was Marcus, huh?" she asked.

"I knew it wasn't Marcus," I lied. "He has no reason to call me."

"I was just checking." Nana smiled and then reclined in her chair.

By the time *American Idol Rewind* had gone off, Nana had dozed off. She was drowning out the Channel 7 news with her snoring, her belly rising and then deflating every few seconds. I gently removed Nana's reading glasses from her face— she wore them when she read the *Chicago Tribune* and also when she watched television—and I placed them on the end table. She didn't budge, and I decided to let her sleep.

I grabbed my phone, started typing Jade a text message.

Hey, ugly...what u doing?

She immediately sent a text back, as if she had been waiting to hear from me.

I sent u a text an hour ago...where u been?

Watchin A.I. with Nana.

Is that how u spendin ur summer vacation...watchin tv with Nana?

Went to a club da other night wit my cuz... adult club...

"Big Things Poppin'," my ring tone of choice, rang loudly through the living room. I quickly silenced it before it woke Nana up. I hit the green button to answer the call.

"Hello," I whispered.

"You are lying!" Jade screamed into the phone.

"Not," I said.

"I need details," she begged.

"Not right now," I said. "Later."

"Nana's sitting right there?"

"Affirmative."

"Then go upstairs, or out on the front porch."

"No."

"Fine, just send me a text, then," she said.

"Cool, bye." I hung up the phone when I saw Nana squirming in her chair.

I sent several text messages and told Jade all about my night out with Sabrina. She was so jealous, and she wished she had taken Nana up on her invitation to spend the summer in Chicago with me. I wished she had, too, because I was dying for some conversation. It was cool hanging out with Nana, but sometimes I just wanted to talk to someone my age, and wanted somebody that I could walk to the BP station with and watch the neighborhood boys play basketball on the corner. It would've been nice to have someone that I could stay up with until the wee hours of the night talking about boys or listening to Chicago's hip-hop station on the front porch. We could've gone to the Ford City Mall and shopped until we dropped—window-shopped, that is.

Nana finally woke herself up with her own snoring, and then looked over at me as if I had done something.

"You still up, sweet pea?"

"Yes, ma'am."

"Well, I'm taking myself on up to bed." She stood; it seemed to take her forever just to get on her feet. She grabbed her glasses and the *Essence* magazine that she had been reading earlier, climbed the stairway to her bedroom.

"Good night, Nana."

"Good night, Indi. Listen for your uncle Keith. He done lost his key again."

"I will, Nana," I said, and then stretched out on the sofa, flipped the channel on the television to MTV. *Run's House* was always a good choice for a late-night laugh, so I settled there. I went into the kitchen in search of a snack and remembered that Nana was a diabetic, so all she had was sugar-free snacks and fresh fruit. I grabbed a green apple from her fruit basket on the dining room table and bit into it. I poured myself a glass of water and headed back to the sofa.

I was startled by my ringing phone and checked the screen to see who it was. Marcus. Guessed he was returning Nana's call from earlier. She had gone to bed, so there was no need for me to pick up the call. I let it roll into voice mail. When I heard the little alert that let me know he'd left a message, I didn't hesitate to listen to it.

"Hey, Indi, it's me, Marcus…. I was just returning your call. Hit me back when you get this message. Peace."

His voice was so fresh and sweet, I had to listen again…and again…and again. Before long, I had listened to Marcus's voice mail message seven times; I resisted the urge to call him back, though. The only thing stopping me was the fact that I didn't have an excuse for returning the call. When he found out that it was Nana who had initially made the call, I'd have to explain why I was calling instead of her. So I passed. Marcus hadn't been at all happy about my idea of the pact, and I wasn't sure if he wanted to talk to me. The night before he'd left for Houston, he didn't even say good-night. There'd been no Skittles thrown against my bedroom window. And when I threw Skittles at his, he didn't even bother to turn on the light. He was done with me, once and for all.

Uncle Keith hadn't knocked on the door yet and my eyelids were getting heavy. I made my way upstairs to my bedroom. The radio on the night-stand next to my bed was tuned to Chicago's station 107.5, and the quiet storm was on. I showered, put on my Victoria's Secret pajamas and hopped into bed. As soon as my head hit the pillow, I realized just how tired I was. Before long I was counting sheep and visiting Snow White's party.

chapter 15

Marcus

I sat in my BMW with the top dropped. *My BMW*—I liked the sound of that. It had a nice ring to it. I pumped the music as I waited for Michelle. If she didn't get a move on, we'd be late for the Lil Wayne concert, and I didn't want to miss one minute of the show. Just to set the tone for the evening, I slipped in Lil Wayne's CD and tested my speakers. The music sounded nice as it drifted into the air, and probably woke up everyone who was sleeping.

Dressed in a pair of tight jeans that looked as if she'd painted them on and a blouse that actually showed cleavage, Michelle hopped into the car. She had left the pop-bottle glasses behind and must have been wearing a pair of contacts. Her hair hung to her shoulders in curls, and I couldn't stop staring at her.

"Let's go, Marcus. We gotta pick up Andre."

I continued to stare.

"What, boy, dang!" she said. "Quit staring at me."

"It's just...you look so different." I smiled at Michelle. "I didn't even recognize you at first. I mean, you actually look...like...like a real girl...."

She rolled her eyes. "Shut up, Marcus, and drive."

I put the car in Reverse and headed out of the parking lot. Every now and then I would glance over at Michelle, just to see if she was real—or to see if she was just a figment of my imagination. I pinched her just to make sure.

"What is your problem?" She squealed when I pinched her. "Stop acting so stupid, Marcus."

"Sorry." I laughed, and then turned into Andre's apartment complex. Before I could blow the horn, he was already heading toward the car, dressed in baggy jeans and a Tall T, with a fitted cap on his head.

"This you, dog?" he asked, checking out the car, and then hopped into the backseat.

"This is me." I grinned. Knew that I was styling and profiling in my new car.

Andre was looking at Michelle as if he didn't recognize her. When she said, "What are you looking at, fart face?" he knew exactly who she was.

"Michelle?" he asked. "Dang, girl! You look like…like a real girl."

"That's what I said." I had to laugh at the fact that Andre and I had the same thoughts about Michelle's new look.

"Both of you are stupid." Michelle pretended to pout and looked out the window. "I knew Andre was stupid, but you, Marcus?"

"Hey, we're just saying that you look good, Michelle. You should take it as a compliment."

"Word," Andre agreed, "that's all we're saying."

Lil Wayne bounced around onstage, his dreadlocks swaying from side to side as he spat out fresh rhymes on the microphone. Girls in the front row were going crazy, screaming, some of them crying. Several of them had their camera phones out in the air and were snapping pictures of Lil Wayne. The music was so loud, and the bass was unreal. Everybody in the house was bouncing to the music.

Dwayne Carter was Lil Wayne's birth name, and

I couldn't help thinking that we were probably distant cousins somewhere down the line. Especially since he was from the seventeenth ward of New Orleans, and my family was from New Orleans. And the fact that he was currently attending the University of Houston really struck me as ironic, since I now called Houston my home. So many similarities, I couldn't wait to corner him backstage and ask him a few questions, find out if we were really related.

Unfortunately, Michelle had misplaced the backstage passes, and we couldn't get past security. She claimed that she'd had them in the back pocket of her jeans when she'd left the house but explained to the security guard that somewhere between her house and the Toyota Center, they must've fallen on the floor.

"Sure they did," he said sarcastically, his body forming a barrier between us and backstage.

No matter what she said, he wasn't trying to hear it.

"Let's just go, Michelle," I said. "It's no big deal."

"It is to me, Marcus." She was almost in tears. "I've been waiting all week just to talk to him. I wanted to get a picture of him with my camera phone. Why do you think I have on these stupid contacts, and this stupid outfit, and got my hair done?"

"I don't know, maybe because that's what normal girls do?" Andre said, and then laughed.

"Shut up, Andre." She normally would've had a comeback for him, but now she didn't even put up a fight.

"Michelle, it's not that serious," I said. "Let's just go."

I was glad I didn't have to drag her out of the Toyota Center kicking and screaming. She left quietly, but I could tell that she was very disappointed. She'd had plans of meeting Lil Wayne face-to-face; probably had a whole speech prepared with things she wanted to say to him. I'd had no idea she liked him that much until that night.

Once in the car, we dropped the top and blasted the music. After everyone had agreed that they were hungry, I pulled the car into a late-night Mexican spot for a bite to eat. In Texas, Mexican restaurants were on every corner, like liquor stores were in the hood. We stepped inside, found a booth and ordered tacos, nachos and enchiladas. Michelle was feeling better about not getting to see Lil Wayne up close and personal, and before long she and Andre were going at it again with their insults.

By the time we pulled into the parking lot of our subdivision, it was almost three o'clock in the morning. Michelle had taken her heels off in the car and was now carrying them in her hand.

"Thanks for driving to the concert, Marcus," she said.

"Thanks for getting the tickets for us. That was cool," I said. "I'll see you tomorrow."

"Okay, Marcus."

I stuck the key into the door and stepped inside. Mom had left the lamp on in the living room, so I turned it off before heading to my bedroom. I changed into a pair of shorts and a T-shirt to sleep in, turned the radio on to the quiet storm. When I checked my phone, I had an unread text message, and I silently hoped it was from Indigo. It read: Thinking of you...Rena.

She had left it hours earlier, during the Lil Wayne concert. No need to respond now, I thought. Instead, I turned on the ceiling fan over my bed and listened to Sade sing "No Ordinary Love."

chapter 16

Marcus

Fourth of July.

Fireworks were illegal in Houston, but I couldn't resist the urge to shoot a few M-80s. Even though they were illegal in Georgia, too, Pop and I still managed to make the drive to Chattanooga, Tennessee, every year and come back with paper bags filled with firecrackers, bottle rockets and M-80s to shoot off in celebration of our nation's independence. Our neighbors usually started popping firecrackers two weeks before the Fourth of July, but Pop made me wait until at least a couple of days before. And late at night on the Fourth of July, after everyone had gone inside and all the evidence had been swept away, Pop and I would sneak out back and shoot our M-80s in the middle of the night. My dog, Killer, would hide underneath the porch with his head covered and howl. I loved to hear Gloria's mouth when she realized that the noise was coming from our backyard. She would be fussing the whole time we were outside, but Pop never gave in, and I was glad. It was the one tradition that we still shared, Pop and I, and he didn't allow Gloria to steal it away.

When I thought of the guy who would soon become my new stepfather, I wondered if he would drive me to a place where M-80s were sold and if he'd shoot them in the middle of the night with me. He didn't seem like the type to buy illegal fireworks, let alone shoot them, even though everybody did it anyway. In fact, he'd probably have me arrested if he knew that I had a bag full of M-80s hidden underneath my bed. I didn't trust him at all.

Mom and I didn't have any traditions together. I hadn't spent much time with her over the years, and definitely not long enough to start any new traditions. But all that would have to change. We'd have to start our own traditions, just like Pop and I had. Today would be a good day to start.

"Ma, what you doing today?" I asked her.

"I thought we might fire up the grill and throw

a few steaks out there. Leon's coming over later," she said. "What would you like to do, Marcus?"

"Well, there's this music festival at the park today. I've been hearing about it on the radio. You wanna go?"

"Marcus, it's hot out there." She frowned. "It's been years since I've been to a concert in the park."

"Well, that's why you should go. You're always working, and never have enough time to just chill," I told her. "Besides, me and you...we need to start a new Fourth of July tradition."

"That's sweet, Marcus, but I've got some work I need to finish up," she said. "I'm gonna pass."

"Okay, Ma, cool." I was disappointed but tried to disguise just how much.

I fixed myself a plate filled with eggs, sausage and toast. Sat down at the bar and ate breakfast as my mother spread paperwork out on the sofa. I noticed that she had taken steaks out of the freezer to thaw, and I figured that our tradition would be to fire up the grill on the balcony and cook them to perfection, and then I'd eat mine alone because she would be too busy working. What an exciting Fourth of July.

When I'd finished eating, I headed for the shower, put on a pair of jean shorts and my Phat Farm shirt and decided to go see what was going on at the pool. There was a community barbecue and pool party scheduled for the day, and I wanted to see if anybody special had decided to show up.

The music wasn't bad; they had someone mixing CDs—it was a combination of old-school and new-school, and the crowd was just as mixed. Old people and young people alike hung out at the pool, talking, swimming and relaxing in lawn chairs. Small children were running about and chasing each other all over the pool area. Somebody's dad had a grill fired up, and some woman placed a tablecloth on a round plastic table filled with packages of hot dog and hamburger buns.

I finally spotted someone I knew—Michelle—and briskly walked toward her. She was sitting on the side of the pool sipping some punch in a plastic cup. A paperback book lay in her lap facedown.

"What you reading, girl?"

"This book my mom bought me," she said. "I'm not much of a reader, but she kept blabbing on and on about these books…. It's a new line of books that are supposed to be about black kids like us, written in our language…yada, yada, yada…"

I took the book from Michelle's lap, lost her page as I looked at the cover. There were two beautiful black girls on the cover—looked like a couple of models.

"Are they girl books?" I asked.

"No, I think they're for everybody."

I turned the book over and read the back of it. The plot sounded very interesting; made me want to read the book.

"How many of these you got?"

"She bought me three of them. I have two more in the house," she said. "Why, you wanna read one?"

"I like the sound of this one," I said, and pulled up a lawn chair next to Michelle, plopped down into it.

"You can't read that one, Marcus. I've already started it, and it's actually pretty good," Michelle said. "I'll go get you the other two out of the house. You can read one of them. But not this one."

"Fine, go get them."

Before Michelle even reached the gate of the pool, my nose was already buried in the first chapter of her book. I was hooked by the first few sentences and found it very interesting that the conversation that the characters were having sounded just like a conversation I would have with my friends. Michelle was gone at least ten minutes, and when

I finally saw her head bouncing down the stairs of her condo unit, I was already on the third chapter. There was no way she was getting this book back. I had to find out what happened next.

I stuck the book into the back pocket of my shorts and took off in the opposite direction of the pool's entrance, headed toward the showers. I hid behind the wall, peeping around the corner until I saw Michelle looking for me. She did this for a few more minutes and then decided to plop down in a lawn chair when she couldn't find me. She opened one of the books that she had in her hand, started flipping through the pages. Soon she was reading. I snuck from behind the wall, headed out of the pool area, across the parking lot and up the stairs to my house. Michelle never looked up.

Mom was still working in the living room, papers spread out all over the sofa and floor, when I passed through. I left her alone and headed for my bedroom. Lying across my bed, I pulled the book out of my back pocket, opened it up and got lost in the pages again. I liked to read, mostly science fiction stories and magazines like *Vibe* and *Sports Illustrated*. I rarely read regular fiction like this. Most of the time the characters didn't look like me, and if they did, they weren't my age and they sounded corny. But I could totally relate to the characters in the book I'd swiped from Michelle. It had me mesmerized, even though it looked like a girl book on the outside—inside, the pages revealed so much more.

Just as I reached the sixteenth chapter, there was a light tap on my door. Mom stuck her head inside.

"What are you doing?"

"Reading this book that I stole from Michelle," I told her.

"It must be pretty good, because I haven't heard a peep from you all day." She had changed into a sundress and had pulled her hair up. "I came to see if you still wanted to go to that festival in the park."

"You serious?" I laid the book down and sat up in bed.

"Yes." She smiled.

"Well, let's go, then!"

I didn't know what had made my mother change her mind, but I was glad she had. I slipped my shoes on and followed her to the kitchen. She'd already packed a cooler filled with Cherry Cokes and bottled water, and she handed it to me to carry. With blankets and a can of Off! to fight off the mosquitoes, we headed to the park.

chapter 17

Indigo

Hotter than July.

That was the name of the Stevie Wonder album Daddy used to listen to when I was a little girl. He had it tucked away in a cabinet that he called his "old-school cabinet." I couldn't even imagine it being hotter than July as I wiped sweat from my face and sipped an ice-cold bottle of water to cool down. I sat in a lawn chair next to Nana, who was singing and popping her fingers to the sounds of Lakeside, an old-school group that was performing onstage.

"Hey now," she said, and moved her shoulders to the music.

I was tired of listening to old-school and wished

that Alicia Keys would hurry up and appear. The radio stations had been hyping up the event all day and had even interviewed her twice on the radio. I'd been waiting for her performance all day. I was hot, and tired of hearing Uncle Keith and Cousin Benny sing the words to every song—off-key. Sabrina had said that she would meet us at Washington Park hours ago, but she hadn't shown up yet, and I was starting to wonder if she was going to show at all. At least if she was there, I'd have someone my age to hang out with. Anything was better than listening to Little Keith ask me a million questions about stupid stuff and pester me to play catch with his football.

Alicia Keys finally took the stage, dressed in a skin-tight pair of silk shorts and high-heeled shoes. She began dancing around and clapping her hands in the air. The crowd followed her lead and started clapping, too. I stood up, just so I could see past the people who were standing in front of us, but it was hard. By the time Alicia started playing the keyboards and singing, I was in a better mood and had a better view of the stage. When she asked us to put our hands in the air, I did just that. And when she sang "You Don't Know My Name," I knew all the words and sang them right along with her. I even began to move my hips.

"You having fun now, Indi?" Uncle Keith asked.

"Yes, I am." I smiled at him.

"That Alicia Keys knows she fine as she wanna be," Cousin Benny said, and then looked over at his wife to see if she'd heard him. She had, and she rolled her eyes.

"Behave, Benny," Nana said, and then wiped sweat from her forehead and sprayed Off! on her bare legs.

"What's up, good people?" Sabrina asked as she walked up from behind, Brittany attached to her hip, sucking on a cherry Popsicle. "Hey, Nana."

Sabrina leaned down, baby and all, and kissed Nana's cheek.

"Hello, sweetie," Nana said, and for the first time that day she seemed tired.

Sabrina looked fly in her denim shorts and red tube top. She wore red sandals and had a new set of microbraids in her hair. She smelled like the fragrance counter at Macy's, and a fresh Coach bag hung from her shoulder.

"Hey, Indi, what's going on, girl?" Sabrina asked.

"What took you so long?" I asked. "I been waiting for you all day."

"I had to wait for Dugie to bring me the car," she said. "Alicia Keys is doing her thing up there. Check her out!"

"I've been waiting for Alicia Keys all day, too. I was tired of listening to old-school."

"Well, the party has arrived." Sabrina sat Brittany on a blanket in the grass. "Come on, Cousin Keith, let's dance."

Uncle Keith and Sabrina started dancing to the music, and it was the beginning of a long day at the park. The fireworks show was the finale, and when it was over, we started packing up blankets, coolers and picnic baskets and headed home.

I was glad to be home; my tank top was stuck to my body from all the sweat. It was nice to step into Nana's and enjoy the air-conditioning. I ran upstairs to my room and checked myself out in the mirror just to see how many shades darker I had become over the course of the day. My neck was sunburned and stinging a little bit. I needed something to rub on my skin, some type of ointment to soothe the burn. I knew Nana would have something in her medicine cabinet—a special cure.

"Nana!" I yelled as the bare bottoms of my feet felt the cold hardwood. "Nana, you got something for sunburns?"

I peeked into her bedroom. She wasn't there, and the bed was completely made. Halfway down the stairs, I could smell something cooking. Wasn't quite sure what it was, but it smelled like barbecued ribs being warmed in the oven. I hoped she had a couple of bones in there for me, because I was hungry, too. I went straight for the kitchen, and Nana was nowhere in sight. I stood there with my hands on my hips for a moment, trying to figure out where she might be. I checked the family room and the front porch. No Nana.

"Nana!" I called out again.

Uncle Keith had dropped us off in front of the house, and we'd climbed out of his old Chrysler carrying lawn chairs and leftover food. He'd said that he was going to drop Little Keith off at home and that he'd be back shortly. Nana and I never held our breath for Uncle Keith to come home; we were usually both asleep by the time he finally made it. We always knew when he was home, though, because the next morning there would be dirty dishes in the sink and all the food from dinner would be gone. There was never any hope of leftovers when Uncle Keith was around.

When I didn't see Nana on the front porch, my heart started beating fast, and I got a little scared. I walked slowly back into the house and stopped in the foyer, thinking about where she might be. I walked back into the kitchen, looked in the oven. Just as I'd thought, she was warming some ribs. I looked out the back window and thought I saw someone lying on the lawn in the backyard. I wondered who it could be as I slowly opened the screen door. I froze when I discovered that, in fact, it was Nana on the lawn. The laundry she'd been pulling from the clothesline was on the ground with her.

I rushed over to her, tears threatening to fill my eyes and my heart pounding out of control.

"Nana!" I screamed.

She never budged.

"Nana!" I screamed again, and then fell to my knees beside her. "Nana, wake up!"

I was afraid to leave her, but knew I needed to get to a phone quickly. I had to call 911. By the time I'd reached the kitchen phone and punched in those three numbers with trembling fingers, there were tears all over my sunburned face.

chapter 18

Marcus

THere were so many people at the park Mom and I had to push our way through the crowd. We strolled past the vendors who were selling their framed art and handmade crafts. There was an artist who offered to draw a sketch of every passerby, and I told Mom that we should have a portrait done. She agreed, and we sat still while he sketched us, capturing every bump and bruise on our faces. When he was done, he turned the portrait around and allowed us to check it out.

"I think it's very nice, Marcus. What do you think?" Mom asked.

"Dude is good." That was all I could say.

He had captured us to perfection, from the

dimples in Mom's cheeks to the waves in my hair. He was definitely an artist, and I wondered why he peddled his work at places like a Fourth of July music festival instead of in an upscale art gallery where he could get paid what his art was worth. He rolled the portrait up and secured it in a cardboard tube, and Mom handed him a crisp twenty-dollar bill.

"Maybe we'll get it framed," she said, and led the way to the next vendor.

We got as close to the stage as possible and laid our blanket out on the ground. There was a group onstage performing Kool & the Gang's old-school song "Get Down On It." Mom instantly started singing along and swinging her hips to the music, her dress swaying to the beat. Everyone around us was singing along and dancing, too.

"Come on, Marcus, dance with your mama!"

I danced but wasn't quite sure how to dance to that type of music. I just followed my mother's lead and moved to it. When she went all the way down to the ground, I went down, too. Before long, we were moving to the same rhythm—Mom and me. She could dance a little bit, had rhythm, and I was surprised. She was in her own little world, and I couldn't remember ever seeing her this way—

actually having a good time, without a care in the world. Whenever I thought of my mother, I thought of a workaholic, with papers spread out all around her. She never had time for fun, because she was always rushing to get back to work.

Pop had always taught me that a hard day's work was good, but you always had to make time to relax and have fun. He said it was okay to do something silly once in a while, just as long as you didn't spend your life being silly. That must have been where he and Mom bumped heads, because she wasn't usually able to relax and have fun. They didn't see eye to eye. Maybe that's why their marriage didn't work out. She was so serious all the time, and meanwhile, her life was passing before her eyes.

I was tired, and collapsed onto the blanket. Mom continued to dance as the band played Cameo's "Word Up." She started doing a dance called the Hustle with a group of people her age. The way they were all moving to the same rhythm, the dance reminded me of the Electric Slide. I sat there for a couple of minutes until I caught the moves, and then I got up and started doing it, too. If anyone could do the Electric Slide, it was me, and the Hustle was nothing more than an old-school Electric Slide, in my opinion.

"I can't believe you're not tired," I said to Mom.

"Boy, I could dance all day long if I wanted to." She laughed. "Back in our day, Rufus and I could tear up a dance floor."

I tried to imagine my father seriously busting a move, and I couldn't. The times I'd seen him dance were rare, and only after too many beers. His stomach hung over his belt now, and if he wasn't stretched out underneath his pickup truck and covered in oil, he was lying back in his recliner in the family room watching the game. He loved listening to old-school music. In fact, every time he set foot in my Jeep, he changed the station and sang the words to every song on the radio. But dancing? I couldn't see it.

"You talking about *my* father? Rufus?"

"The one and only, baby. Rufus was a good dancer," she said, still moving to the music. "Of course, that was when he was much younger and a few pounds thinner."

"Yeah, you haven't seen Pop in a minute. He's got the Dunlop."

"The Dunlop? What's that, Marcus?"

"You know, his midsection looks like a Dunlop tire."

"Marcus, you are so silly." She laughed so hard she ended up finally collapsing onto the blanket.

I sat down beside her and popped the top on a can of Cherry Coke.

"You want one, Ma?" I asked.

"Gimme a bottle of water, baby."

By the time the sun had set and darkness approached, the show that I'd waited for all day began. Mom and I already had the best seats in the house as the fireworks bolted across the sky, making either a whistling noise or a loud pop. I looked over at Mom, who was smiling and enjoying the show. She hadn't looked at one stack of papers for at least four hours, and I was glad.

By the time we made it home, it was late, and I just knew Mom would rush to her bedroom, change into her pajamas and pass out for the night. She stood thoughtfully in the middle of the floor.

"We can still throw those steaks on the grill if you want to, Marcus," she said.

"I'll get the fire started," I said, and rushed out onto the patio before she changed her mind.

I stood on our patio next to the grill, got it fired up while Mom marinated the steaks in her special spices. By the time she brought them outside, the grill was hot and smoke filled the air. The steaks sizzled when she placed them on the heat. It didn't take long for them to cook, and before I knew it, she was pulling the meat off with tongs. She quickly tossed a salad and warmed some French bread in the oven.

We sat down at the dining room table, said grace and then dug in. We ate and discussed our Fourth of July tradition—a tradition that had begun that day.

"What are your thoughts about a person shooting an M-80 on the Fourth of July?" I asked.

"What are you talking about, Marcus?" she asked. "I think a person who shoots an M-80 on the Fourth of July is breaking the law. Why do you ask?"

I dug into my pocket and pulled one out.

"Marcus, what are you doing with that?" Mom eyeballed the firework.

"It's a Fourth of July tradition to pop at least one M-80 before the night is over."

Mom shook her head. "Go ahead, just make sure that nobody sees you," she said.

I grabbed a book of matches from the kitchen drawer, stepped out onto the balcony. Looked toward both ends of the parking lot, just to make sure nobody was outside watching me. I lit the stem of the M-80, threw it and covered my ears as it exploded with a loud *bang!*

"Give me one of those, boy." Mom stood in the doorway.

I dug into my pocket and handed her an M-80. She lit it, threw it into the air and covered her ears. This went on until all twenty of them were gone. She lit one and then I lit one, and each time, we covered our ears and ducked just in case somebody was trying to figure out where the explosions were coming from.

When I stretched out across my bed for the night, I had to smile at the thought of having such a good day with Mom. I'd made her happy, and that made me smile. I grabbed the Kimani TRU book I'd been reading, opened it up to the page where I'd left off and read until I could no longer hold my eyes open. The Fourth of July had new meaning.

chapter 19

Indigo

I stared at the television that was mounted in a corner of the emergency room. A *Seinfeld* rerun was on, but I wasn't really watching. My eyes were burning because I'd cried during the entire ride in the back of the ambulance with Nana. She hadn't responded to anything the paramedics had tried, and all I could do was pray. I prayed that God wouldn't take my grandmother from me; I wasn't quite done with her yet, and she still had so much to teach me—about life, about all sorts of stuff. Besides, Uncle Keith needed her, too. Even though he was a grown man, he still needed Nana. Everyone did.

God, if you do this one thing for me, I promise

to behave myself and to do what I'm told. I won't back talk Mama or mumble things under my breath when she gets on my nerves. I'll keep my room clean without being told. I'll try harder in school and will never ever sass Mrs. Kennedy again. God, please help me. I know I haven't been the best kid, but I promise to try harder. Cross my heart and hope to die, stick a needle in my eye... Amen. I wasn't sure if He heard me, but I sure hoped so.

When Uncle Keith and Cousin Benny rushed into the ER, I knew that they were just as scared as I was. Cousin Benny spotted me and they headed my way. I had no news for them, and that really bothered me. After the nurses had rushed Nana back to one of the rooms on a stretcher, I'd been told to have a seat in the waiting room and that someone would come and talk to me soon. It had been an hour since then, and there still wasn't any word on Nana's condition.

"Your grandmother's going to be just fine," a woman had said when we'd arrived at the hospital. "Do you have a family member you can call, sweetheart? Grab yourself a cup of hot chocolate. Someone will come and talk to you soon."

That was the last I'd heard from anybody, and my

stomach hadn't stopped turning flips. I hugged Uncle Keith when I saw him, and the longer I held on, the quicker the tears streamed down my face.

"It's okay, Indi. Nana's gonna be just fine," he said as he wiped tears from my soaking-wet face, and I believed him. "I'm gonna go see if I can find something out."

I watched as Uncle Keith walked across the room. He spoke a few words to the woman behind the Plexiglas window. I couldn't hear what the woman said to Uncle Keith, but he folded his arms across his chest and waited while she made a phone call. He stood there, a look of worry on his face, a wrinkle in his forehead as he lifted his baseball cap and scratched his head. He had the same wrinkle in his forehead that my daddy often got when he was stressing out about something. They were alike in so many ways, yet so different. My daddy was more a disciplinarian, while Uncle Keith was so cool and down-to-earth. But they both loved their mother to death. I'd called Daddy earlier while I waited in the ER. He was worried, I could tell, but kept it together for my sake. He kept calling me to see if there was any news on Nana's condition, but I wasn't able to tell him anything. I promised to call him the minute I had some news.

A few minutes after the woman hung up the phone, the double doors swung opened and a gray-haired man wearing green scrubs and a white doctor's jacket walked through them. He said a few words, and Uncle Keith's head bounced up and down as he listened. I wondered what was being said but waited until Uncle Keith gave Cousin Benny and me a signal to join him and go behind the double doors and into the ICU, where Nana was.

We rushed toward him, and he instantly wrapped his arm around my shoulder as we followed the gray-haired doctor. Uncle Keith didn't say a word, and I wondered where we were going and what we would find once we got there.

"What did he say?" I whispered to Uncle Keith.

"He said that your nana is a very strong woman and that she's going to be fine."

"For real?"

"For real." Uncle Keith planted a kiss on my forehead and eased my fears just a little bit. He didn't say that Nana would be coming home with us, and that probably meant that she was worse off than I could've imagined. If God had had intentions of taking Nana away, he could've at least given me a warning.

Nana's eyes were just barely open, but she attempted to smile when we entered the room.

"Hey, sweet pea." She struggled with every syllable. "How you doing?"

"I'm doing just fine, Nana. What about you?"

She held her hand out and reached for me, and my heart pounded when I saw that fluids were being pumped through an IV in the back of her hand. I moved closer to the bed.

"You scared me, Nana…. I didn't know what to do." Tears filled my eyes as I held her hand in mine.

"You needn't worry about me, sweet pea. I'll be just fine." She smiled. "Your nana is strong."

When I heard Nana say it, I actually believed it, and I finally exhaled for the first time that night.

"I got here as soon as I heard." Sabrina rushed into the room and straight toward Nana's bed. She grabbed Nana's free hand and kissed her cheek. "You gave me a scare, Nana."

"I'm doing just fine," Nana said before drifting into a light sleep, her stomach moving up and down beneath the covers. The doctors had given her something to help her sleep.

"We should go and let her get some rest," said Uncle Keith.

"I wanna stay." I expressed my desires quickly.

"I can spend the night with Nana so she doesn't have to be alone."

"I don't think you can sleep in here, Indi," said Cousin Benny. "They have strict rules in the ICU, baby girl."

"Can we ask?" I couldn't leave Nana alone. I wanted to stay with her, just to make sure she was all right. I had always taken care of Nana, monitoring what she ate and making sure she did the right things. She needed me.

Unfortunately, the hospital staff disagreed. They were convinced that they could take better care of Nana than I could. And even though the doctor had assured us that Nana was out of the woods, I was still skeptical. Nobody had witnessed her just a few hours ago laid out on the lawn like that, except me—an image that would forever be burned in my memory.

"Uncle Keith is right, Indi. We should let Nana rest." Sabrina grabbed my hand and pulled me toward the doorway. "You can come home with me until Nana's better, if you want to."

I thought about the alternative—being in Nana's big old house all by myself, hearing those noises all through the night. "The house settling," Nana would say. "Nothing to be afraid of, sweet pea."

"I think that would be a good idea, Indi," Uncle Keith said, knowing that he probably wouldn't show up until the crack of dawn, if at all.

I kissed Nana on the forehead and prayed she would be home soon. As the nurse began to check Nana's vital signs, I followed my family out of the room and down the hospital corridor. Grudgingly.

chapter 20

Marcus

A left-hand layup sent the ball soaring into the basket with a swish. The last two points, and that was all we needed to reach twenty. I glanced over at Michelle and Andre, who were sitting in the bleachers, and they gave each other a high five. The bass from somebody's loud music caused everyone to turn around and look; it came from a silver Monte Carlo backing into a space in the parking lot. Cedric stepped out of the car, wearing white shorts and a wrinkled black T-shirt, his hair in cornrows. Two of his boys followed. He pulled his shirt over his head and tossed it into the bleachers, headed toward the court.

"I got next," he said to no one in particular, and

nobody seemed to have a problem with it. I instantly knew he was a bully, the way he came on the scene and demanded his place.

El tossed the ball to Cedric, and he passed it off to one of his boys to take it out. Cedric brought the ball downcourt, and within seconds he was standing right in front of me, bouncing the ball from side to side for a ridiculously long time, a mean sneer on his face. I reached in to snatch the ball away, but Cedric was quick and moved to my right, took the ball to the basket and tossed it in—an easy two points. El got the rebound and tossed it to a tall, slender dude on our team. Tall and Slender took the ball out and tossed it to me.

I hustled downcourt toward the basket, and before I knew it, Cedric was in my face again—the same sneer on his face. It was almost as if he was focusing all of his energy on guarding me. When he pushed me, I didn't see it coming.

"Man, what's your problem?" I asked.

"I ain't got no problem," Cedric responded, and then pushed me again.

I pushed back and then we were rolling around on the pavement. In seconds El was pulling me off Cedric and one of Cedric's boys was holding him.

"Cedric, what's up with you?" El asked.

"This fool is supposed to be messing with my girl!" Cedric spat through bloody lips.

"Everybody knows that Rena's your girl, Ced," El said. "What's your beef with Flash?"

I wanted to know the same thing, and waited to hear Cedric's response. There was no doubt I liked Rena. I thought she was fine; everybody did. Rena and I had gone to the beach together, and shared a kiss, but that was it. Besides, according to her, she wasn't his girl, anyway. In my opinion, that made her fair game.

"My beef is that Rena belongs to me, and this fool has disrespected me, crossed the line." Cedric wiped blood from his mouth, smeared it across his white shorts.

"That's not what she told me," I said, and pulled away from El's grasp. I started walking away, headed toward Michelle and Andre, who were in the middle of the crowd that had gathered for the fight. "Let's go, y'all."

"Marcus, you okay?" Michelle asked, and tossed my shirt to me. She pulled a Kleenex out of her purse and began to rub blood from a cut on my face.

"I'm cool," I said, and wiped my face with my shirt.

The three of us headed in the opposite direction of the crowd.

"You can have her, punk! She's tarnished now," Cedric yelled. I flipped my middle finger into the air and kept walking. "I hope you enjoy being a daddy, fool."

I stopped dead in my tracks, confused by Cedric's comments. What was he talking about, "I hope you enjoy being a daddy"? Laughter followed his comments, and he continued with his foolish talk.

"You better learn how to change diapers.... Waaa...waaa...waaa." He made noises like a baby crying, and sounded so juvenile.

I couldn't shake what he said, so I turned to face him, headed his way.

"What are you talking about, man?"

"Oh, you mean she didn't tell you?"

"Tell me what, fool?" I asked.

"She didn't tell you that she's pregnant?" Cedric laughed sarcastically. "And that you the daddy?"

"That's not possible," I said, and seriously had to rethink my actions toward Rena. I knew that I hadn't had sex with this girl. Either she was crazy or a huge liar. Either way, she had me in a bad situation. "I never touched that girl."

"That's not what Rena's claiming, punk!" Cedric said.

"We'll see," I said, and walked away again.

"Yeah, we'll see!" Cedric yelled.

Michelle, Andre and I cut through backside of the Diamond Shamrock store and walked through the parking lot of the Shell gas station. I walked briskly ahead of them, my mind on nothing but finding Rena as soon as possible.

"Is that true what Cedric said, Marcus?" Michelle asked.

"I never touched that girl," I said through clenched teeth, never turning to look at Michelle. "All I did was kiss her. And I never knew anybody that got pregnant from kissing."

"That's not what Rena's going around telling people," Andre chimed in. "She's telling people that y'all are knocking boots, dog."

"I heard that, too," Michelle said.

"You heard what, Michelle?" I was suddenly in her face.

"I heard that you and Rena, you know...that y'all were having sex." She didn't back down.

"And you believed something stupid like that?" I asked, still in Michelle's face.

"Don't be mad at me, Marcus. I didn't start the rumors," Michelle said.

"But you listened to them." I pointed my finger right at Michelle's forehead.

I walked faster, right into traffic as I jaywalked across the busy street. The horn from a U-Haul blared as the truck rushed toward me, swerving to keep from hitting me.

"Don't blame us because you didn't wear a condom, Marcus!" Michelle bellowed across the street.

That took my anger to another level.

Rena wasn't on her throne when I made it to the pool area. She was nowhere in sight, and I wondered where she was when I needed to confront her about the lies that were spreading like wildfire.

"Where's Rena?" I asked her redheaded counterpart.

"She's sick today," he said. "She'll be back tomorrow."

I didn't say another word, just headed toward Rena's building. I had to get to the bottom of this, and today. I took the stairs two at a time until I reached her unit. I banged on her door. When nobody answered, I rang the doorbell. Still no answer. Just as I turned to walk away, the door slowly crept open.

"Hey, Marcus," Rena said softly.

"Rena, we need to talk," I said.

She looked terrible. Her hair was all over her head, her eyes were bloodshot and she was dressed in wrinkled pajamas.

"Can it wait, Marcus? I don't really feel well today."

"Rena, I just left the basketball court. Your boyfriend, Cedric, was there."

"Ex-boyfriend," Rena corrected me.

"Whatever he is, I just got into a fight with him...over you and your stupid lie...."

"What lie?"

"Well, apparently you're going around telling people that you're pregnant, and that I'm supposed to be the father," I told her. "Rena, you know that we never..."

Rena pulled me into her house.

"Marcus, who else knows about this?" she asked.

"Everybody who was at the court today."

She sighed long and hard. Tears rolled down her face, and I wrapped my arms around her, hugged her until she got herself together. Then I followed Rena into the living room. A black-and-white portrait of Rena hung over the fireplace, and lots of other black-and-white framed photos covered the brick-red walls. I found a seat on the edge of the black leather sofa.

"I did a home pregnancy test two days ago, and

it was positive. I accidentally left the box in the trash can in my bathroom, and my mother found it. She and my father started grilling me about it...asking me if I was pregnant. I finally fessed up...told them yes. Of course my daddy wanted to know who the father was, and I wouldn't tell him. He kept asking me if it was Cedric."

"Well, is it?" I asked.

"Yes, but I can't tell my father that, Marcus. He would kill Cedric. He hates him. That's why we broke up, because my father forbade me to see him. He said that Cedric is a thug and a good-for-nothing drug dealer."

"Is he?"

"He's not that bad. He came from an abusive home and moved out when he was fifteen. He's lived on his own since then. And so he's had to make a living somehow."

"There are legal ways of making a living, Rena. And selling drugs is not one of them."

"I know that, Marcus. I did as my father asked me to.... I broke up with Cedric. But I still loved him...at least, I thought I did, until you came along. I really like you."

"I like you, too, Rena. But why did you tell Cedric that I'm your baby's father?"

"Because I couldn't tell him the truth. He would demand to be involved in this pregnancy, and my father's not having that."

"Who does your father think you're pregnant by?"

Rena gave me a sheepish smile.

"What? You told your father it was me?" I asked, standing now. "What did you do that for?"

"Because you're such a great guy, with values and stuff like that. You're from a decent home," she said.

"He'll be trying to kill me, too."

"He won't, Marcus, I promise," she said. "Can you play along? Just for a little while?"

"Until when?"

"Until I have a chance to take care of it," she said. "I'm getting an abortion."

I brushed my hand across my waves, shook my head. I was nervous about this whole scheme of Rena's. Taking claim of a baby that didn't belong to me was downright crazy; it was something I needed to think through.

"I don't know, Rena...."

"Please, Marcus," she begged. "I have an appointment at the abortion clinic next Tuesday. Just until then."

"And what happens on Tuesday? How will you clear my name?"

"I'll tell my father the truth. If there's no baby, then he has no reason to kill Cedric."

"Of course not, he'll be looking for me instead."

"I promise this will work out, Marcus."

I felt uneasy about the whole thing, but I agreed to play along until Tuesday. I walked toward the front door, and Rena followed.

"Thank you, Marcus," she whispered.

"I'll holler at you later," I said, and opened the door.

"Hey, Marcus...one more thing..."

"What's that?"

"Can you take me on Tuesday?"

She was asking a lot from one guy, but I couldn't leave her out there alone.

"Yeah, I'll take you."

"Thank you."

I didn't say another word, just walked slowly down the stairs and into the bright sunshine.

chapter 21

Marcus

I parked in the most inconspicuous space I could find in the parking lot, as far away from the door as possible.

"I'll just wait in the car," I told Rena.

"You sure?"

"Positive."

"Okay. It shouldn't take long." Rena stepped out of my car, the bill of her baseball cap down over her eyes. She wore sweatpants and a tank top.

I watched as she walked slowly to the door, and just before she went inside, she gave me a look over her shoulder. I gave her a smile of reassurance and then she stepped inside. I should've gone in with Rena; that would've been the manly thing to do.

But I didn't want to be seen in a place like this, a place where babies' lives were ended before they even had a chance. It wasn't something I wanted to be involved in. Just the thought of ending a baby's life made me sad. It wasn't the kid's fault that things were this way, so why should he or she be punished? It wasn't my call, though. I was simply the driver. I had no say-so in this situation whatsoever. That was my position, and I was sticking to it.

I sat in the parking lot for at least an hour, sunk down in the driver's seat of my car, listening to Young Jeezy's CD. By the time Rena finally tapped on the window of the car, I had fallen asleep. I hit the power locks and she got in.

"Well?" I asked.

"Well what?" She was different.

"How did it go?" I asked.

"Let's just go, Marcus," she said.

I started the car and pulled out of the parking lot of the abortion clinic. There was total silence on the way home. She didn't want to talk about it, and I didn't make her. I was just glad that the whole experience was over with. Wanted Rena to be the happy free spirit she'd once been. I figured that something like this might change her forever, though.

I pulled into my usual space in the subdivision. I sat there for a moment, thinking that Rena might want to talk. But she didn't. Instead, she eased out of the car and slowly walked toward her house. She didn't even say goodbye, and I didn't pressure her. I just shut off my engine, hopped out and headed up the stairs.

When I walked into my house, Mom was on the phone with one of her girlfriends, gossiping about something. I walked right past her and rushed to my room, shut the door behind me. I heard Mom say, "Girl, let me call you back. Something's wrong with Marcus."

It wasn't long before she popped her head into my room.

"Hey, Ma," I said.

"Marcus, what's wrong?"

"Nothing," I lied. I wasn't ready to share this type of news with my mother.

"Baby, we need to talk," she said, then stepped inside and sat on the edge of my bed.

Had she heard the news, too? That I was supposed to be the father of Rena's baby, when I hadn't even done what it took to earn that title? None of it mattered anymore, anyway. Rena had taken care of it, and the nightmare was over now. She'd promised to tell her father the truth and clear my name so I could have my reputation back. Only irresponsible dudes found themselves in situations like this. It wasn't that I didn't want to make love to a beautiful girl like Rena, but I would've taken precautions to be responsible and safe.

Mom's little talk was interrupted by the doorbell.

"That's probably Leon," she said, "but why is he ringing the bell when he has a key?"

She had given him a key? Had he already moved in and nobody told me? I followed her and popped into the kitchen for a Cherry Coke.

"Are you Mrs. Carter?" The man on the other side of the door had an unfamiliar voice. It definitely wasn't Leon. This guy stood at about six feet, three inches tall. A full beard covered his face.

"Yes, I am," Mom said.

"May I come in?" he asked. "I'm David Jordan, Rena's father. She's a friend of your son's."

"Oh, yes, I've met Rena. Come on in," Mom said, and let him inside. Rena was right behind him, her head hanging low. "Hello, Rena. How are you?"

"I'm fine, Mrs. Carter," she said softly.

"This is my son, Marcus," Mom said to Rena's father. "Marcus, do you know Mr. Jordan?"

"No, we've never met."

I held my hand out to shake Mr. Jordan's, but he didn't reach back. Instead, he dismissed me and focused his attention on my mother. "We have a problem, Mrs. Carter."

"Let's step in here and have a seat." Mom led them into the living room. The three of them sat down. I stood in the doorway of the room, curious as to what was about to go down. "What seems to be the problem?"

"I'll just get straight to the point. My daughter is pregnant. And she says that your son is the father."

My heart was pounding out of control. Clearly there was a mistake, because Rena and I had just left the abortion clinic, and she'd promised to clear my name.

"Marcus, is this true?" Mom asked.

"No." I said it straight up.

"Are you calling my daughter a liar?" Mr. Jordan stood. He wanted to get in my face, but he remained composed. "She told me that it happened right here in your house, Mrs. Carter. Now, I don't know what kinda crap you allow to go on up in here, but you need to get your house in order."

"Mr. Jordan, I don't appreciate you coming into my home making accusations about my son," Mom defended me. "We're prepared to have a DNA test."

"Mom, no, we're not," I pleaded. "There's no need. I know I'm not the father. Rena, tell your father the truth."

She never opened her mouth to say one word, and I was confused.

"I understand that you took her to an abortion clinic this morning...forcing her to end this pregnancy," he said. "We are Catholics and are totally against abortion. How dare you—"

"Marcus, is this true?" Mom asked. "Did you take Rena to an abortion clinic this morning?"

"Yes, I did but—"

"How could you do this, Marcus?" Mom looked as if I'd betrayed her.

Mr. Jordan's piercing eyes stared my way. He was furious. Rena held her head low, not once defending me as she had promised, and I was caught in a terrible circle of lies and deceit.

"I would just like to know what Marcus is prepared to do about this situation, Mrs. Carter," Mr. Jordan said.

"My son is a very responsible young man, and if he has to step up to the plate, he will." My mother escorted Mr. Jordan to the door.

"You're darn right he will," Mr. Jordan said, and he and Rena left.

"Marcus, give me the keys to your car," Mom said after Mr. Jordan was gone.

"Are you serious?" I asked her.

"As a heart attack."

I didn't say another word, just dug into my pocket and tossed her the keys to my BMW...or *her* BMW. She never once asked me if the baby had been mine. I was guilty in her eyes, and it hurt. There was no need to plead my case to my mother, so I left it alone. Just like Nana Summer told me once, everything would come out in the wash.

When the doorbell rang, Mom opened the door and let Leon in. He was the last person I needed to see. I didn't need to be judged, and he had judgment written all over his face. He would take my mother's side in a heartbeat. There was no expressing myself—I was guilty before I even had the opportunity to explain. I headed for my room, thought about packing my bags and heading back to Atlanta. Houston was no place for Marcus Carter.

chapter 22

Indigo

I borrowed a pair of Sabrina's shorts and some high-heeled shoes. I wanted to look grown when we showed up at the club. And there was nothing grown-up about my wardrobe. It wasn't that I didn't have cute clothes, but for this new lifestyle of mine, I needed fresh new stuff. The kind of stuff Sabrina wore, the kind Dugan appreciated.

"Indi, you look fly," Dugan said when I stepped into the living room.

"Thank you." I smiled.

Sabrina and I stepped into the club and were immediately swept away to the dance floor. I bounced to a Jay-Z tune with my handsome dance partner, who kept me on the floor for at least three songs after that.

"My name is Larry," my partner announced when we finally abandoned the floor. "What's yours?"

"Indigo."

"Can I buy you a drink, Indigo?" he asked.

"Maybe a glass of wine," I said.

I wasn't sure what type of drink to order, considering I wasn't a drinker. I just knew that I didn't even like the smell of beer, so that was not an option. Mama had an occasional glass of wine when company came over, and there were special times when she had let me taste hers. Wine seemed to be the best choice.

I knew that wine was a drink that needed to be sipped, and so I sipped slowly. It had a bitter taste, much more dry than the wine that Mama drank, and not sweet like berries. I frowned every time I took a sip but forced it down just to save face. Larry sipped a beer as we sat at a cozy table in the corner of the room, discussing why his babies' mama had left him and taken the kids with her. Larry had already had two beers, and I hadn't even finished half of my wine. The longer it sat, the warmer it became. And warm dry wine was much worse than chilled dry wine. I left my drink on the table as Larry pulled me out onto the floor again. We fell in with a crowd of people who were doing the Cupid Shuffle.

Back at the bar, I slipped onto the seat next to Sabrina, who was way too cozy with a man who looked twice her age. They were laughing about something, and suddenly his lips brushed against hers, and I prayed that Dugan was nowhere around. She didn't even notice that I was there as this man's fingertips caressed her face. She grabbed her beer, took a drink and continued her conversation with him.

"Brina, you ready to go?" I asked, and she swung around and looked at me. Her eyes bloodshot, she smiled.

"Hey, there's my cousin!" she shouted, and that was when I smelled the alcohol on her breath. "Meet my cousin Indi. Indi, this is...uh... What you say your name was?"

The man laughed and moved closer to her ear. "Stan."

"Yeah, this is Stan. Indi, meet Stan." Sabrina's speech was slurred.

Stan reached over Sabrina's shoulder and shook my hand.

"Nice to meet you, Indi," he said. "What you drinking?"

"Nothing. I'm fine," I answered, and really became concerned about how we were going to get home. It was obvious that Sabrina wasn't able to walk to the door, let alone drive. And I didn't have a license—only a permit that allowed me to drive as long as there was an adult in the car. Sabrina was seventeen, and hardly an adult. We had a problem, and I didn't have a solution. How could Sabrina drink so much, knowing that she didn't have a designated driver? She had placed us in an awkward position.

Outside, we stood in the parking lot while Sabrina searched her purse for the keys to Dugan's car. She wasn't able to find them, and I was glad, because it gave me more time to come up with a plan. I did not feel safe getting in the car with Sabrina. I'd heard the reports about people driving drunk, and I wasn't ready to become a statistic. I had my entire life ahead of me. Unfortunately, I'd have to do what I knew was the right thing—call Uncle Keith and ask him to pick us up. It was the only option. I pulled my cell phone out of my purse and started slowly dialing his number.

"This is Keith.... Leave a message at the beep."

I didn't bother to leave a message. The keys to the car jingled as Sabrina held them in the air.

"Indi, you gotta drive."

"What?"

"I can't do it, girl. I had way too much to drink."

She wasn't telling me anything I didn't already know. How was I supposed to drive us home when I didn't even know my way around Chicago? I snatched the keys from Sabrina, unlocked the doors and told her to get in the car while I asked for directions. She did just that, and her head rolled around on the passenger's headrest. I flagged down a couple who happened to be leaving the club, gave them Sabrina's address and asked for directions. They told me how to get there, and I hopped into the driver's seat.

I adjusted my seat and mirrors the way Daddy had taught me. I checked my purse to make sure I had my fake ID that Sabrina had arranged for me. It was there. I was nervous even about putting the car in Reverse. This would be my first time driving a car without Daddy being on the passenger's side, barking out orders. "Stay in your lane, Indi.... Start pumping your brakes before you get to the light.... Watch the car in front of you, and don't follow so close behind."

This time I was doing it all by myself, and the thought caused my hands to shake as I held on to the steering wheel. I backed out of the parking space slowly, carefully, and then pulled out onto Michigan Avenue just as carefully. I started pumping my brakes as I approached the stoplight and came to a complete stop. It wasn't a smooth stop, and Sabrina and I jerked as the car eased just behind the white line. She had fallen asleep and didn't even wake up when I swung the car around the corner much too fast. Instead of pressing the brakes, I accidentally accelerated and found myself in the middle of an intersection. Sabrina's car collided with another car that was traveling in the other direction, and my head bounced against the steering wheel.

"What happened, Indi?" Sabrina asked, raising her head for just a moment.

"Sabrina, I hit somebody!" I yelled.

"For real?" she asked.

"Yes!" My heart pounded.

I jumped out and walked toward the other car. The woman driving seemed to be out of it, and there were two small children in the backseat. I didn't know what to do. I knew that the police should be called, and maybe paramedics, too, but I couldn't think straight.

"Indi, come on, we gotta go! We can't stay here," Sabrina yelled from her window.

"We have to call the police," I told her.

"If we call the police, we're going to jail," she said. "Indi, come on. We gotta go."

I couldn't leave the woman there with her children, not knowing if she was all right. There was an awful feeling in my stomach.

"We have to make sure these people are okay, Sabrina," I said.

"We'll call the police once we get farther down the road. We can't wait around for them," Sabrina said. "You don't even have a driver's license. Do you want to spend the night in jail and call your father in Atlanta to come and pick you up?"

She did have a point. And as long as we sent help for the family, I was fine. I hopped back into the driver's seat and fled the accident scene, Dugan's car breezing through the South Side of Chicago.

Once in the apartment complex, I put the car in Park and sat there for a moment, just trying to get my breathing to an even pace. Sabrina and I stepped out of the car.

"Yo, Sabrina...." A familiar voice rang through the parking lot, and I turned to see who it was. Dugan walked toward us and wrapped his arms around Sabrina's waist. His eyes found mine. "Y'all cool?"

"Hey, baby," Sabrina said, and kissed Dugan's lips.

"She's been drinking," I told Dugan.

"Indi, stop telling all my business. I'm straight," she said, holding her Baby Phat purse close to her chest as if she had a million dollars in it.

"Come on, Sabrina, let me get you in the house," Dugan said. He held on to Sabrina just to keep her from falling, and I followed close behind.

He opened the door to the apartment and ushered Sabrina inside.

"Did y'all have fun?" he asked.

"It was okay," I said.

I didn't bother to tell Dugan that we'd fled the scene of an accident. He didn't know that I was so nervous at that moment I thought the world around me was going to collapse. I wanted to go back to see if that woman and her kids were okay. Once we had gotten farther down the road, I had called 911 and told them that an accident had occurred. I asked them to hurry to the scene because there was an injured woman with her children. When the operator asked me for my name, I hung up the phone.

Dugan took Sabrina into their bedroom, and I stood in the middle of the living room, wondering if my sleeping arrangements would be same as they had been the last time I'd spent the night. There were only two bedrooms in the apartment; one belonged to Sabrina's baby, and the only bed in it was a crib. Dugan must've read my mind, because when he came back into the living room, he was carrying a blanket and a pillow.

"Welcome to the guest bedroom, Indi. This is all we got right now. You can sleep on the couch like before, or you can make a pallet on the floor." He handed me the blanket and pillow.

"I'll take the couch."

I went into the bathroom and changed into my Victoria's Secret pajamas, the ones with PINK written across the chest in white letters. I sat on the couch and pulled the covers up to my chin. When Dugan's hands touched my shoulders, I thought I was dreaming. He began to give me a massage, pressing his fingertips into my shoulders. His lips brushed the back of my neck and I froze. When his fingertips began to wander toward my breasts, I jumped clear off the couch and stood.

Dugan moved toward me and pulled me close to

him. He tried kissing my lips, but I turned my head, pulled away.

"What's wrong?" he asked, holding on tighter. "Ain't you feeling this?"

"No."

"Yes, you are, Indi. I see how you look at me when Sabrina's not around."

"I see how you look at me."

"Okay, so I'm guilty.... I think you're beautiful," he said. "Is that a crime?"

I didn't answer.

"I want you, Indi," Dugan whispered in my ear.

"No," I said. "Please stop."

"You know you want this." He pushed me onto the sofa and pressed his body against mine.

He had me pinned down, and I couldn't move; he was too heavy.

"Please stop!" I begged.

His mouth covered mine in an unwanted kiss.

"Dugan!" Sabrina's voice startled me.

It must've startled him, too, because he got up and moved toward Sabrina, trying to explain his actions.

"Baby," he said.

"What were you doing?" Sabrina asked Dugan.

"Teaching your little cousin here a lesson. She

was all up in my grill, and I was tired of it. Ever since the barbecue, she's been checking me out...."

I couldn't believe he was saying all these things about me, making up lies. And Sabrina was standing there looking as if she believed him. I was furious. I wanted to slap some sense into her drunk behind and let her know that her boyfriend was a disgusting pervert.

I ignored their conversation and dialed my uncle Keith's number. When I got his voice mail, I left a message this time. "Uncle Keith, as soon as you get this message, can you please come and pick me up from Sabrina's? Please hurry...."

I walked out of the house and nobody even noticed I was gone. I found refuge on the back steps as I prayed for Uncle Keith to receive my message sooner than later. I thought of Marcus and wondered what he was doing. If he were here, he'd rescue me from this nightmare that I was in. He'd know just what to do. I was so busy trying to be a grown-up that I'd made all kinds of bad choices in one night. I realized that all I really wanted to be was a teenager again. I wanted to be sixteen, with a curfew and a boyfriend who loved me.

I dialed Marcus's number for the first time all summer and hoped that he answered.

chapter 23

Marcus

when I saw Indigo's number flash across the screen, I thought I was dreaming. It was two o'clock in the morning, and I wondered if something was wrong. I picked up.

"Hello."

"Hi." Her voice was soft and sweet, like music to my ears. Then it sounded like she was crying. "I miss you so much, Marcus."

"Indi, what's wrong?"

"Everything."

"Like what?"

"Well, for starters, Nana's in the hospital. She went into a diabetic coma on the Fourth of July."

"Nana's in the hospital?" I asked.

"Yes, and I had a car wreck tonight—"

"Indi, you can't drive. You don't even have a driver's license."

"I know that, but my cousin Sabrina was drunk and couldn't drive us home. So I had to drive, Marcus, and I hit this woman and her kids," she said, "and...I don't even know if they're all right...."

"What do you mean you don't know if they're all right? Were they okay when the cops got there?"

"I left before the cops came."

This caused me to sit up in bed. I'd been sound asleep when I'd heard T.I.'s "Big Things Poppin'" ring tone sound throughout my bedroom.

"Indi, you fled the scene of an accident?"

"It was either that or go to jail. All I had was my permit and the fake ID that I used to get into the nightclub."

"Nightclub?"

"Yeah, we went to a real nightclub, Marcus, with real drinks and cigarette smoke everywhere," she said, "and...my cousin's grown boyfriend just tried to molest me."

"Are you serious?" I asked. "I'll kill him!"

"It's okay."

"Where are you now, Indi?"

"Sitting on the back steps of my cousin's apartment complex...praying that my uncle Keith gets here soon."

"Is he on his way?"

"I left him a message."

"Indi, I'm worried about you," I told her. "I'm coming to see about you."

"How, Marcus?"

"I'll get there, Indi. Some way, somehow, I promise."

I didn't know how, but I had to find a way to get to Indigo. She needed me. I rushed to the kitchen and found the Yellow Pages, looked for the listing of airlines and began calling them one by one, in search of the cheapest flight from Houston to Chicago. When I finally found a good one, I packed my suitcase.

Mom's purse was lying on the kitchen counter. I searched her wallet for a credit card—any one of them would do. I pulled her American Express out of its little compartment, booked my flight, which was leaving in two hours. I scribbled a note for Mom, told her not to worry and that I would call her later. I stuck the note on the refrigerator door, stuffed three hundred dollars into Mom's purse and eased the front door shut as quietly as possible.

I knew Michelle's window was on the east side of the building because she talked about being able to see the tennis courts from her bedroom. I counted the floors until I was able to determine which window was hers. I tossed a Skittle at her window. Nothing. I tossed another one, and still nothing. When I tossed the third one, the bedroom light popped on. Michelle poked her head out the window and looked disappointed when she saw it was me.

"What do *you* want?" Her greeting told me she was still a little salty about our argument the other day. I'd hurt her feelings and never really apologized.

"I need your help," I said anyway.

"So?"

"So, can you take me to the airport? I'll give you some gas money."

"What, Marcus? You're losing it."

"I'm serious."

She scanned the sidewalk, saw my luggage resting against the curb. "Are you crazy?"

"I have an emergency."

"Why should I do this, Marcus?" She was backing down, softening up a little bit.

"Because I'm your friend, that's why." I was reeling her in.

"Are you...my friend?"

"Forever and always," I said.

She thought about my request for a moment. I stood there, my luggage on the sidewalk.

"I'll be down in a minute, Marcus." Michelle shut her window and was downstairs in record time.

She insisted that Andre go along for the ride, just so she wouldn't have to drive back home by herself, so we stopped by and picked him up. The three of us drove down the highway in Michelle's old Kia Sephia with the two missing hubcaps. At three o'clock in the morning, 50 Cent was rapping in our ears. She didn't have much bass in her speakers, but she had the stereo pumped as loud as it could go and the windows rolled all the way down because she didn't have air-conditioning. The three of us were hyped at the crack of dawn and discussed everything that had taken place over the course of the summer.

"I thought you were gonna stay, Marcus, and go to school here," Michelle said.

"That was the original plan. But after I thought about it, Houston is no place for me," I told her, "and my mom really doesn't have room for me in her life. She has her new husband-to-be, Leon."

"She's going to be pissed about you leaving like this, Marcus," Andre said, "without saying good-bye."

"I know."

For the first time, reality had set in. I had to admit, the way I left was wrong. But I was angry at the way my mother had handled the whole Rena incident. She hadn't even given me a chance to explain my side of the story. She'd already had me changing diapers and warming formula for a baby that wasn't even mine. Pop would've at least heard my side, given me the benefit of the doubt first. But Mom didn't even do that. Aside from all that, Indigo needed me. Her situation was much more serious than mine, and I needed to be there for her, to rescue her. That was my job.

I couldn't believe that I would actually see her beautiful face in just a matter of hours. I missed her so much, and hoped that she was ready to let go of this stupid pact—a pact that should never have been made anyway. And I needed to check on Nana Summer, make sure she was all right. My decision to leave was an important one, and I would just have to face the consequences later. But for right now, I had an electronic ticket to Chicago O'Hare airport waiting for me, and I couldn't be late.

"Marcus, you hurt my feelings the other day,

when you snapped at me for no reason," Michelle confessed. "That wasn't even cool."

"I know, and I'm sorry. I wasn't trying to hurt you. I was just upset."

"I don't know why you wasted your time on a girl like Rena anyway."

"Me, either," I said. "I hope she'll be happy."

"Me, too," Michelle said.

In front of the airport, Michelle pulled her car up to the curb. I immediately hopped out and pulled my luggage out of the trunk.

"I'm gonna miss you, Marcus," Michelle said. "Thanks for being my friend."

"Anytime," I told her, and put her in a headlock.

"Will you keep in touch?" She almost had tears in her eyes and started getting all mushy.

"Of course. I got the digits," I told her. "Take care of Andre here."

"I will." She smiled. "Especially now that we've decided to go out."

"You mean go out as in boyfriend-girlfriend go out?" I asked, shocked.

"Yeah, silly!" she said.

"That's right, dog. I think she's hot," Andre said. When he placed his arm around her, I knew they were serious.

"Wow" was all I could say.

Andre and I gave each other dap.

"Take care of her, bro," I told him, "because if you don't, I'll have to come back to Houston whip your behind."

"It's been real, Marcus," Andre said.

"No doubt."

I waved goodbye to my friends as I stepped through the automatic doors. Michelle and Andre had definitely made my summer worthwhile.

My head was filled with thoughts of Indigo as I squirmed in my seat. Excitement rushed through me when I felt the wheels of the plane hit the runway and the pilot announced that we were in Chicago. As the plane taxied to the gate, I pulled my cell phone out to see if I had any missed calls from Indigo. She had left me a text message:

Uncle Keith picked me up.... Come to Nana's house.

As the cab sped through the streets of Chicago, I took in the sights. I'd never been to the state of Illinois, but it seemed to be an interesting place. Chicago was a big city like Atlanta, with huge buildings and long highways. Nana lived on the South Side, in a neighborhood filled with huge brick houses that had been built many years ago. As the cab slowed at the curb, I looked up at the two-story house and knew I was just seconds away from seeing my favorite two girls in the whole world. Before I had a chance to step out of the car, Indigo was standing on the porch waiting for me. Her hair was a wild mass on her head, and she wore khaki shorts and a tight-fitting T-shirt.

A half smile on her face, I wondered if she was just as excited to see me as I was her. Whatever exhaustion I'd felt from being up all night seemed to disappear the moment I saw her. I paid the driver, pulled my luggage out of the trunk of the cab and made my way up the stairs. No words were spoken between Indigo and me; I just held her in my arms. I didn't want to let go. If letting go meant that I'd risk losing her again, then I wanted to hold on forever. I kissed her lips and knew right then that our pact was over.

chapter 24

Indigo

when I saw Marcus, everything bad that had happened seemed to disappear. For a moment, I forgot all about the accident and about Dugan trying to take advantage of me. As always, Marcus showed up and was there for me. In just a matter of hours, he'd managed to fly all the way from Houston to Chicago, just to rescue me and to give Sabrina's boyfriend, Dugan, a black eye. That was all Marcus kept talking about—how he was going to punch Dugan in the face and make him wish he'd never put his hands on me.

Sitting on the back steps at Sabrina's apartment, I'd had time to rethink my entire life as I prayed that Uncle Keith would receive my message. He had received it, and when he pulled up out front, I sighed long and hard and rushed to his car. I didn't feel like explaining what had taken place. I just snapped my seat belt around me and looked straight ahead.

"You okay, Indi?" Uncle Keith had asked.

"I'm fine now," I told him. "Thanks for picking me up."

"Did something happen in there? Did Sabrina do something to you?"

"No," I simply said.

I began to stare out the window, and Uncle Keith let it go, didn't ask any more questions. He just drove us home to Nana's house in silence, and I was grateful because I really didn't want to talk about it.

I peeked in at Nana, who was home from the hospital and resting in her bedroom. I wanted to wake her up, because I really needed a hug. I needed to talk to her, tell her all that had gone on and ask her if I'd done the right thing. I wanted to know if I could have handled things better. She looked peaceful as her stomach moved up and down and light snores escaped from her mouth. I decided to plant a kiss on her forehead, and then pulled her door shut before creeping downstairs.

* * *

I had pancake mix all over my face, the counters and the floor as I mixed it up in a bowl. I knew that Marcus would be arriving soon and wanted to cook him breakfast. It was a challenge without the assistance of Nana, who made the best pancakes I'd ever had in my entire life. I stirred the batter and dropped vanilla flavoring into it before spooning it into the hot skillet. Although they were a little burned around the edges, I hoped they tasted better than they looked.

"And just what do you have going on in here?" Nana asked, standing in the doorway of the kitchen in her robe.

"I'm making breakfast. What are you doing up?"

"I smelled something burning." She laughed.

"I can't make them like you, Nana. Can you help me?"

She didn't answer, just grabbed the batter and stirred it a bit. She made nice round pancakes and cooked them until they were golden brown. They weren't like mine, lopsided and burned, and I was grateful that she had taken over. I felt guilty for not making her get back into bed. She had no business in the kitchen flipping pancakes while recovering from a diabetic coma. I wanted to stop her, but I couldn't bring myself to. The vanilla aroma was floating through the air, and I knew it would be only moments before Marcus pulled up.

After he gave Nana and me hugs and kisses, I escorted him to the kitchen, where I had cooked pancakes, sausages and scrambled eggs. I loaded a plate filled with all of it and slid it in front of Marcus.

"Aren't you gonna eat?" he asked.

"No, I just want to watch you eat."

And that was exactly what I did. I watched as syrup drizzled down his chin, and I realized then how much I'd missed him.

After breakfast, Marcus insisted that we take a cab ride over to Sabrina's apartment. He claimed that he wanted to have a conversation with Dugan. I had no idea that he really had intentions of roughing Dugan up until we pulled into the complex. We knocked on the door, and when Dugan swung it open, Marcus looked at me.

"This him?" he asked.

"Yes," I said, and before I knew it, Marcus had Dugan in a headlock.

"Marcus, stop!" I yelled.

Dugan's breathing was heavy as Marcus let him go.

"Man, what's your problem?" Dugan asked Marcus.

"You're my problem," Marcus said. "If you ever put your hands on my girl again, you won't live to tell anybody."

"Well, tell your girl to stop making advances toward me and we won't have this problem again."

I glanced at Sabrina, wondered if she believed that I had made advances toward Dugan or if she knew the truth—that he was a sleazebag. I couldn't read her face at first.

"Indi, you've caused enough trouble here," she said. "I think you and your boyfriend should just leave."

I couldn't believe she said that. She couldn't possibly have believed that I was the one who'd betrayed her. And if my gut instinct was right, I wasn't the first person Dugan had done this to. What hurt was the fact that she believed him over blood kin. Sabrina and I had been family a lot longer than Dugan had been her boyfriend. We had history. We used to play in the water sprinklers together and eat peanut-butter-and-jelly sandwiches in her backyard. We'd received the same whippings, and watched Tom and Jerry on the Cartoon Network more times than I could remember. And she was asking me to leave.

I didn't hesitate to step out into the hallway and tramp down the stairs of the apartment complex. As I stood in the middle of the parking lot, I knew that I would never return to this place. Marcus followed and pulled his cell phone out to call the police. They were there instantly. The heavy white officer jotted down all the details of the incident and then headed up the stairs toward Sabrina and Dugan's apartment. Later, Dugan was being escorted out the door, his hands behind his back in handcuffs. Sabrina was close behind, her daughter on her hip with a bottle hanging from her mouth.

Sabrina was in tears as Dugan sat in the backseat of the police car. As it turned out, Dugan had outstanding warrants for his arrest. Aside from a drug trafficking charge, apparently he'd also sexually assaulted a woman just a month earlier. The woman had filed a report, and the police had been looking for him ever since. I guess they found their man, thanks to Marcus and me.

I felt sorry for Sabrina as she stood there watching her man being escorted to the Cook County jail. Even though I hadn't forgiven her yet, I felt sorry for her. She had placed me in a bad situation by forcing me to drive us home because she was too drunk to remember her own name. I felt bad about the family that I'd hit. Marcus insisted that we do the right thing and go down to the police department and explain what had taken place. Luckily, they let me off with a warning and told me that the family was doing fine. I was happy to hear that. Dugan's insurance was going to cover the damage to their car.

Sabrina was my older cousin who I had looked up to most of my life. She'd always been much prettier, a much better dresser and better dancer than I was. Her grades had always been exceptional, when mine were just mediocre. She had the hottest boyfriends and her life was always more exciting than mine. Until this trip to Chicago, I had wanted to be Sabrina. But looking back, I discovered that I just wanted to be Indigo Summer, an average girl, with an average life, wearing average clothes, making average grades and doing average things. I didn't have any babies, and my boyfriend was an exceptional guy who cared about me.

Nana was standing in the doorway when we made it back, her hands on her hips as she tapped her foot against the floor.

"Somebody want to tell me what's going on?" she asked. "Sabrina just called over here hysterical because they were hauling Dugan off to jail…said

something about you having something to do with
it...."

I hadn't planned to share any of this with Nana.
She didn't need to be involved in the situation; she
needed to recover instead of worrying herself to
death. But she wanted an explanation, and I wasn't
about to avoid giving her one. She might have been
sick, but she was still my Nana, and still had the
power to rearrange my behind.

"Dugan's on his way to jail because he tried to
molest me."

"What?" She was appalled, and even more so
when I told her all that had gone on.

I told Nana about going to the nightclub and
how Sabrina was so drunk that she wasn't able to
drive us home. I told her about the car accident and
how Dugan had forced himself on me.

"I bet Sabrina didn't tell you that the cops were
looking for Dugan because he'd sexually assaulted
someone else," I said to Nana.

"No, she didn't tell me any of that," Nana said.
"I'm sorry you had to go through that, baby. I love
Sabrina to death, but I knew that she was bad
news."

"And there I was wishing that I had her life. It
seemed so exciting, Nana."

"The grass always looks greener on the other side of the fence, Indi, but that's not always the case. You make the best of what you have, and that's all you can do," Nana said. "You're still young, and you'll go through many more lessons."

I nodded in agreement. I knew that there would be plenty more experiences just waiting to happen in my life.

"And what's your story, young man?" Nana asked Marcus. "Why are you in the Windy City and not in Houston?"

"Indigo called me, and when she told me what happened, I had to come and rescue her," Marcus explained.

"So you came to save the day." Nana smiled and nodded. "And do your parents know where you are?"

Marcus dropped his head, looked sheepish.

"I left a note."

"You left a note." It was more a statement than a question, and Nana was no longer smiling. "You got ten seconds to get your mama on that phone and let her know where you are. And then I want to speak with her when you're done."

"Yes, ma'am," Marcus said.

"I don't know what I'm gonna do with you two." She was smiling again.

Marcus dialed his mother's number and began to explain where he was, and why. I could hear her yelling from clear across the room, and I feared for his life. I knew he could handle a lowlife like Dugan, but handling his mother was a different story.

chapter 25

Marcus

It was hard explaining to Mom that I had high-jacked her credit card but that I had done it with good intentions. Once she stopped yelling and calmed down, I was able to explain my side of the story. She was still upset, but at least she wasn't yelling anymore.

"I received a phone call from Rena's father," Mom finally said. "He says that you're not the father of the baby."

"I told you that, Mom."

"Why did you lie about it in the first place, Marcus?"

"Because Rena asked me to play along. Her father hates the guy who is the real father."

"So you decided to take the fall for someone else?" she asked.

"I was protecting Rena," I explained.

"I'm sorry for not believing you, son. It's just that..."

"It's okay."

"Your father has done a wonderful job with you. He's helped you to become quite a man. I'm not sure if I can do such a good job." The tone in her voice was much softer now. "Are you planning to go back to Atlanta?"

"Yes, ma'am. I think that's where I belong," I said softly. "Are your feelings hurt about that?"

"Well, I will miss you," she said, "but I want you to be happy, Marcus."

"I'm glad that you found Leon. He seems pretty cool. I always hoped that you and Pop would get back together, but since that never happened, I'm glad you found someone you love."

"Thank you, Marcus. It means a lot that you approve of him," she said, "and I want you to visit again next summer."

"Oh, most def. I'll have to come back and check on Michelle and Andre, see what they're up to."

"Then it's a deal! You'll spend the summers with me." She was happy, and that made me happy.

"And every Fourth of July, we'll continue our tradition."

"That sounds good, Ma."

I thought about our day in the park, when Mom was shaking it up and having a good time. Shooting M-80s was the highlight of the evening, and I looked forward to doing that again.

"How are you planning to get back to Atlanta? Do I need to purchase you a ticket?"

"No, ma'am. Indigo's father is picking us up and taking us home. He'll be here soon."

"Is she the girl that you're *not* getting serious about? The one who caused you to steal your mother's credit card, book a flight to Chicago, just to rescue her?"

"That's her."

"She must really be special."

"She is." I found myself smiling as I stole a glance at Indigo, who was across the room yapping with Nana. If I had to, I would rescue her again...and again...and again. She was special, and I was glad the summer was coming to an end so that we could get back to the way we were. No more pact, no more Rena. Just me and Indi. I couldn't wait to throw Skittles at her bedroom window and wake her up on a Saturday morning when she was trying to sleep in. I couldn't wait for her to prop her feet up on the dashboard of my Jeep on the way home from school. I couldn't wait to take her to the old airport, watch the planes land and count the stars. I couldn't wait to meet her at the creek behind her house and plant kisses all over her face.

My summer in Houston hadn't been half-bad, but I was eager to get back to the ATL.

chapter 26

Indigo

I didn't know what Marcus had done during his summer vacation in Houston, and I really didn't want to know. All I wanted to know was that our stupid pact had ended and that we could go back to where we left off. As we sat in Daddy's pickup truck, our fingers intertwined, I knew we both were in for trouble when we got home. Marcus's mother had been worried sick about him, and she was upset about him leaving in the middle of the night and using her credit card to book a flight to Chicago. Mr. Carter wasn't happy, either. In fact, when Marcus spoke with him on the phone, I could hear him yelling on the other end of the phone and threatening that Marcus would be grounded until he was twenty-one. After all the yelling, he was happy to learn that Marcus had changed his mind about living in Houston with his mother. Marcus told his father that his home was in Atlanta, with him and Gloria. And even though he didn't like Gloria that much, he had gotten used to her, and that was much better than breaking in a new step-parent.

Marcus discovered that Mrs. Carter's fiancé, Leon, had had plans to send him to an all-boys' school in some rural part of Texas, where he would have shared a dorm with hundreds of other boys and would only come home on the weekends and during holidays. Marcus had thought that his mother genuinely wanted him to live with her, particularly since she'd missed so much of his life a child, but the truth was she wasn't ready to be a full-time mother. She didn't know how. Marcus didn't hold it against her; he simply made a vow to visit her during his next summer vacation. She was cool with that.

We both had learned so much over the summer—about life and about ourselves. As we blew kisses at Nana, who was standing on the front porch in her robe and slippers, I thought about the night I'd found her unconscious on the back lawn. She was doing much better, but I still worried about her. Uncle Keith slipped his arm around her shoulder and they both waved to us. I made him promise to take good care of her. Even though Nana wanted him to move out and get his own place, I was grateful that he didn't. Without me around, she needed somebody to keep an eye on her.

As we approached the stop sign at the end of the block, I glanced up at Jordan Fisher's house. He was outside throwing a Frisbee back and forth with his little brother. Our eyes locked for a long moment, and I wondered how things might have been if we'd bumped into each other earlier in the summer. I wondered if he would've been my summer boyfriend again.

I gave Marcus's hand a tight squeeze. Who needed a summer boyfriend when I had Marcus Carter?